CODENAME PERSEUS

Stephen Filkin was born in Scotland in 1964 but was raised in the South of England. At the age of 17 he moved to London where he gained experience in casual jobs ranging from assisting in an acupuncture clinic to postal sorting. He began to write for television and magazines until, on the advice of a friend, he turned his hand to writing novels.

In CODENAME PERSEUS he displays a remarkably detailed knowledge of the intricacies of the internecine struggle in Northern Ireland, and, as the story unfolds, vividly brings to life the characters of both the hunters and hunted.

It is Mr. Filkin's first book and although he is currently reading for a degree in Contemporary Studies there is a rich promise of more to come.

CODENAME PERSEUS

by
Stephen Filkin

BULLFINCH PUBLICATIONS

Published by
BULLFINCH PUBLICATIONS,
245 Hunts Cross Avenue,
Woolton, Liverpool 25.
Tel/Fax: 051 428 1284

ISBN 0 9522722 1 0

Designed and produced by
Coveropen Ltd., Wigan. Tel: 0942 821831

Printed and bound in Great Britain.

THE PLAYERS

PIRA ARMY COUNCIL:	Martin Kennedy (Chief of Staff) Patrick Wheelan Christy Keegan Eoin McCann Dermot O'Shea Michael Donovan Tom Gallagher
PIRA BRIGADE COMMANDERS:	Jim O'Hara Gerry Kavanagh Danny Malahide Rory Maguire Paddy Lynch
PIRA ACTIVE SERVICE UNIT:	Tim Reilly Jimmy Gilvarry Peter O'Connor Ricky Farrell
PIRA A.S.U. LIAISON OFFICER:	Donal Brady
PIRA A.S.U. WELFARE OFFICERS (MAINLAND):	Patrick Kelly Seamie McGee
WILD CARDS:	Sean O'Malley Cleary
MI5 'K' BRANCH:	Harry Thomson (Director) Jamie Daniels
G INTELLIGENCE (ARMY):	Colonel Harris
'A' BRANCH (WATCHER SERVICE):	Bill Smith Jackson
MI5 ULSTER:	Frank Davis
THE PERSEUS LINKMEN:	Alan Pennick (Major, G1 Army Intelligence, ret'd.) Peter Wilcox (Captain, 22 SAS, ret'd.)
MINISTRY OF DEFENCE:	Emily Baker
WILCOX'S TEAM:	Jacko Tyler (22 SAS, ret'd.) Charlie Kane (22 SAS, ret'd.) Dizze Greaves (Royal Marines, ret'd.) Mike Travis (Parachute Regt., ret'd.)

In the burrows of the Nightmare
Where Justice naked is,
Time Watches from the shadow ...

W.H. Auden

PROLOGUE

THERE were seven of them in the farmhouse kitchen, grouped around the polished pinewood table.

"For God's sake!" cried Patrick Wheelan. "When are ye gonna wake up an' realise what's happenin' here? The bloddy army is pickin' our people up like shit on their shoes an' we're doin' nothin' about it!"

"What can we do?" asked Christy Keegan, a corpulent, balding solicitor with pebble glasses.

"We can bloddy well fight back!"

"Our problem's not with the army," said Eoin McCann, easing his spare frame into a more comfortable position. "It's with us. Someone in the Movement's in bed with the Brits an' until we find out who it is, it's pointless tryin' to fight bloody anyone."

Wheelan slumped back into his chair and glowered. Of all the members of the PIRA Army Council, he was the least inclined to patience.

Dermot O'Shea leaned forward in his seat and clasped his hands across the table. "We know we've been compromised and we know the leak must be way on high in light of the quality of information the Security Forces have received. Our source in Lisburn — "

"Gave us some cock-and-bull story of an operation that's nine years old!" said Michael Donovan, a tall loose bull of a man with lank brown hair who had voted against O'Shea's election to the Army Council on the grounds that he was more committed to the dollar than the Cause.

"The discovery of three arms dumps and a safehouse last month," O'Shea replied, his skinny forefinger rapping the table for emphasis. "An SAS ambush on one of our cross-border operations resulting in the deaths of six of our men. They're facts! Everything points to a high-level penetration."

"So what do you suggest we do?" asked Keegan.

"Scale things down for a while. Give ourselves time to find the leak and plug it."

"An' you believe whoever it is'll still be standin' while the rest of us are lyin' down on our backs with our feet in the air?" Donovan asked, his gravelly voice dripping with contempt.

"No one said anything about lying down," O'Shea replied evenly. "We have our contact in Lisburn. He can give us everything we need. But one thing's for certain – we can't keep on the way we are – we're too damn near the edge of the cliff and one more push could send us over."

The room fell silent. Martin Kennedy, the Chief-of-Staff, a man of fifty with silver hair and a lazy waistline, raised a questioning eyebrow at Tom Gallagher, the crippled survivor of the premature explosion of a bomb he had planted in Belfast City Centre.

"An' what about you, Tom?" he asked. "Have you nothin' to say?"

Gallagher shrugged. "I agree with Dermot insofar as we can't operate effectively until we find an' nail the tout. But we can't suspend all operations while we look for him. We've too many balls in the air."

A murmur of agreement, then Kennedy held up a silencing hand.

"Dermot?"

O'Shea lowered his eyes reflectively, and when he finally spoke it was as if it were to himself.

"Since we're on a runaway bus, I suggest we put pressure on our source in Lisburn. We get the names of the tout's handlers and information regarding their present whereabouts. Then we send in teams to lift them, take them someplace nice and quiet and keep them there till we get what we're after – the name of the bastard who's shafting us. That way we can carry on as normal while we work to shut down the flow of information."

"Or keep the pipeline open, bait a trap," Keegan added. "Their info's been so good up to now, they'd be apt to act on it without thinking. That way we could really hit them! By the time they realised they'd been had, we'd have done more damage than we've ever done before!"

"So it's agreed, then?" Kennedy asked. "We go for the handlers?"

It was agreed.

When they had gone, Kennedy entered the small sitting room. It was furnished without extravagance and had oak beams exposed in the low, smoke-stained ceiling. A man stood by the window. He was dressed casually in a three-quarter length tan leather jacket and faded jeans.

"Well?" asked Kennedy.

"Could be any one of them."

"So, what d'you suggest?"

"O'Shea's idea was a good one," the man replied. "Squeeze the Lisburn contact an' take it from there."

Kennedy went to the fireplace and poked life back into the coals. The red glow gave his face an almost demonic look and when he straightened up it was evident that the fire had only emphasised what was already there.

"I want this bastard, Donal. I want him t'pay for what he's done. Get in touch with our man in Lisburn. Get him t'give ye all he's got."

The term 'our man' was something of a misnomer. Gambling debts which had been bought by the IRA could only be used so far as a lever and were hardly likely to guarantee repayment to the extent which Kennedy required.

"An' if he refuses t' co-operate?"

"Tell him we'll inform on him for helpin' us in the past," the Chief said, turning back to stare into the fire. "An' if that's not enough, ye can tell him that when he gets out o'prison there'll be a plot o'land waitin' for him with his headstone sittin' on top of it."

In spite of the heat, it seemed as if a chill had entered the room. It was evident that the interview was over and the man called Donal quietly stepped out into the night, pulling the door to behind him and his collar up close about his neck. Had anyone chanced to see him they would have thought that he looked troubled. And they would have been right. For he was the man whom Kennedy sought; he was the man whom the Brits had compromised, sending him back as a traitor to the Cause, with the codename Perseus and a lifespan which had suddenly gone into overdraft.

He hurried down the track to where his car was parked from sight in the bushes, urgently considering how he could get himself safely removed from the game before he was discovered. And he would be discovered: he knew that. It was only a matter of time ...

For now, at least, he was safe, he was trusted. Kennedy was seeking him among his synod of terror, and the irony of being chosen to set in motion the operation to find himself almost made him smile.

Almost ...

Climbing into his battered Cortina, he keyed the ignition and slowly drove away. Before him was the road to Belfast and behind him lay nine years of lies and treachery against everything he had once believed in, held as sacred.

CHAPTER 1

IT was six o'clock on a Saturday morning when Peter Wilcox peeled himself reluctantly from the cot in the corner of his office. He had only had three-and-a-half hours sleep and in the metal bin beside his paper-burdened desk lay the debris of a six-pack and an empty bottle of scotch. He rose unsteadily and, drawing back the curtains, winced as daylight clawed his eyeballs through the grimy basement windows; then he stumbled into the tiny kitchen which occasionally served as a bathroom where he rinsed away the crust and fug of sleep.

He stared into the shaving mirror balanced on the sill. The man he saw was dark-haired, going grey, with deep blue eyes veined like a roadmap, and worn features scored by thirty-six years of neglect. He was a little under six feet tall, with a good build starting to lose its definition, and on his chest and upper-left back were two puckered scars to show where the bullet had ripped through his lung and ended his career as a captain in the SAS: a souvenir of his final tour in the Land of Ire.

He filled the kettle and returned to the office where he pulled a clean but crumpled shirt from a drawer in the filing cabinet. Putting it on, he punted the blanketed body on the floor beside him.

"Come on, Jacko. Off your arse."

The response was muffled, but clear enough to make him smile.

"Piss off, can'tcha? M'bleedin' 'ead's killin' me!"

"Will be if I forget you're there and step on it," Wilcox replied.

With a theatrical groan, the body moved and the blanket fell away to reveal a short, hairy, ugly little cockney, with a straggly 'tache and the frame of an emaciated whippet.

Jacko Tyler had been a trooper in Wilcox's unit when he took that bullet through the lung. The Intelligence clowns in Lisburn had fucked up and a team led by Wilcox had been sent into bandit country to foil the mortaring of a cop shop. The Provos had been waiting and in the firefight three terrorists had died. Wilcox had been caught by a stray round and Jacko, who had packed his wounds to stop the bleeding and punched him with a syringe of morphine, had kept him alive until the cavalry had arrived. That had been four years ago and Wilcox had the scars and a divorce to remember it by.

"Whassa time, anyway?" Jacko asked through a yawn.

"Time you got up off the floor and went back home to your wife."

When the kettle boiled, Wilcox made a brew. When he returned to the office, Jacko had dressed and was sitting behind the desk.

"Time you got crackin' with this lot, innit?"

"If it bothers you that much," Wilcox replied, handing him a steaming mug, "why don't you do it?"

"Nah, s'officer's work, paperwork; 'sides, you're the brains of the outfit."

The 'outfit' was a small and fairly profitable security firm they had dreamed up nearly a year ago. Anyone with plenty of money and afraid of being turned over because of it could rely on them for sound advice and discount security devices — well, Jacko's brother-in-law *was* in the trade. The firm had five bodies, altogether — another ex-SAS man, a marine and a para — and their pool of knowledge regarding covert entry and other related techniques had so far proved the master of the average scally with a bag marked swag.

Of course, their talents led them into other, shadier areas. But nothing too illegal, although at times the rewards were almost irresistable.

"Brains, huh?" Wilcox said. "I'll remind you of that next time you disagree with one of my decisions."

"When 'ave I ever disagreed with you?"

"Where do you want me to start?"

"Ow about 'ere? You can clear a space so I can put me bleedin' mug down."

Wilcox scowled. Jacko grinned, then drowned his 'tache in the mug. He was right, of course; the paperwork did need some attention. But then, there was always Monday ...

"Well," said Jacko, dropping the mug on the sill behind him and rising. "It's 'igh time I pissed off. Angie'll 'ave your balls for keepin' me out this late."

"Tell her to buy a stronger apron," Wilcox returned lightly. "And while you're at it, lose the 'tache. Business is tough enough without you scaring the fish away. You look like an extra from a ravioli Western."

Jacko replied with a two-fingered salute, then disappeared through the doorway with a grin and up the steps to the street. For a security man he was bloody careless, Wilcox mused, closing the reinforced door. But then, it was just another item to add to the ever-growing list of irritations he was forced to suffer from the lackadaisical talent he employed.

He finished his tea and slumped down at the desk. In the far left-hand corner almost hidden from view by stacks of paper was a silver-framed photo of his ex-wife Jenny and ten-year-old son David. Leaning across, he picked it up and blew away the dust. The end of another month already? The days had seemed to melt away. He put it back, then rose and pulled on his jacket. The drive to Lindfield would take him just over an hour and, locking the office door behind him, he drove to his flat in Ealing where he showered and changed his clothes.

Lindfield was a smallish village in rural Hampshire. Some of it old and most of it new, it was not a candidate for the tourist handbooks, and Wilcox felt a familiar distaste as he cruised along its spoiled environs.

Jenny's parents had moved here after the War. In those days it had been an Eden with customs which had long died out; and though they had adapted with the change, it was evident that they found it a disgrace. Wilcox had once asked them why they stayed and was given the answer he might have expected. Their roots were here, firmly embedded, and anyway, they weren't getting any younger. Jenny's roots were here, too, which was why she had scuttled back after the divorce. Now David's were sunk, he went to school and had his friends here; and with everything so neatly resolved, it was Wilcox who was the outsider.

He parked before a small neat gabled house, with a small lush square of grass cut in half by a concrete driveway, and killed the engine. Fifty yards away was a field with a couple of horses browsing, totally unconcerned by the racket of a mixed, pre-teen gang playing soldiers; and beside the field, almost hidden from sight behind a bank of trees, came the mechanical roar and clanging progress of a new and uniform housing project rising from scarred foundations.

Wilcox cut across the lawn and stopped before the newly-varnished door where he thumbed the bell. A moment later it opened and Jenny's mother, Marjory, cooed her delight and hugged him tight, which made Wilcox feel warm inside as he knew she really meant it.

"Peter, darling, you look ravishing!"

"Not so bad yourself," Wilcox replied, finishing the ritual.

"Come on in. I'll tell David you're here."

She bustled off and he entered the living room to find Jenny's father, Tom, seated in a chair pulled up to the fire. He struggled to his feet, dressing gown falling open to reveal a pair of thick blue cotton pyjamas, and stretched out his hand.

"Hallo, son, you gave me quite a turn. I thought you were that quack who's been killing me off."

Tom was sixty-seven, with hollow cheeks and a pale complexion topped by a mat of unruly grey hair. He had worked as a moulder in a nearby plastics factory and was seriously affected by thirty years exposure to the fumes.

Wilcox shook his hand. "Last I heard it was the other way about."

"Well, how in the hell can you trust a doctor who can't even look after himself?" He chuckled. "Seriously, though; he only pops in now to take my temperature, so I must be on the mend."

It was a lie — they both knew it — but Tom was an easy- going man who knew that dwelling on matters which could not be fixed could only make bearing them harder.

Then Jenny entered wearing a light summer blouse and tight jeans. Her shoulder-length fair hair was pulled tightly back from her face into a bun and her eyes were slightly bruised from sleepless nights.

Tom winked. "Time for my rub."

When he had gone, Wilcox asked: "How is he, really?"

"Doctor Markham said it's too early to tell. But it's serious."

"And Marje? How's she coping?"

"You know mum," Jenny replied, "she bottles things up. I think she needs a break."

Wilcox nodded. It can't have been easy on any of them. For a while they stood in silence. Then he said. "I've missed you." But before she could reply, the living room door flew open and a blur raced in and jumped into his arms.

"Hello, Dad!" it cried.

After lunch they took the labrador for a walk. They wandered down Canes Lane and David let him off the lead.

The portly beast scampered after him and soon they were out of sight around the bend and into the trees.

"He's been looking forward to this all week," Jenny said with a smile. "Where are you taking him this time?"

"Sailing on Fenleigh Mere."

"He'll like that."

"Why not come along?"

She shook her head. "David sees enough of me. He needs some time with his father."

He could have been mistaken, but to Wilcox's ears she had made 'father' sound like 'stranger'.

"Why have you stopped?" she asked.

"Isn't that what people normally do when they walk into a wall?"

"I don't know what you mean."

He was pretty certain that she did, but decided it was neither the time nor the place for going into it. Besides, David was calling for them. They carried on down the path to the bend, crossed the narrow stone bridge in single-file and into the trees. The shallow river stretched before them and behind the bushes lining the far bank, the foul breath of the sewage farm drifted on the warm afternoon air.

It was only later that night when David had finally been persuaded into bed that Wilcox decided to find out what was eating her. Experience had taught him that the best way of handling her was the direct one. She had no time for the scenic route where matters of importance were concerned – indeed, her natural candour was one of the things which had first attracted him – but the ground had to be chosen with care; and Marjory, whose antennae had been quivering since the protagonists had returned from their walk, suggested they go to that 'darling little pub' with the tree which had grown through its roof.

An hour later, they were sipping their drinks beneath a willow tree in the beer garden. The sun was sinking and although it was still warm, Jenny pulled her cardigan tight and leant back in the plastic chair with her arms folded defensively.

"I think it's time you told me what's on your mind," Wilcox said, cutting straight to the chase. "Ever since I came you've been behaving strangely."

"Does that surprise you?"

"Frankly, yes. If I've done something wrong I'd like to know what it is and get it cleared up as quickly as possible."

"David says he wants to be a soldier."

"What?"

"He wants to be just like his Dad, a bloody hero."

"And how long's this been going on?"

"If you spent more time with him you wouldn't have to ask."

"It was you who got the court to restrict my access to one bloody visit a month."

"Which you didn't fight."

"Things were bad enough – I didn't see the point in making them worse."

"You didn't even come for his birthday!"

"I telephoned, sent him a present!"

"Which he only opened a fortnight later because he was so bloody upset!"

Their raised voices were attracting attention from the other tables. Wilcox shuffled uncomfortably and avoided Jenny's glare. Commissioned at eighteen and married at twenty-five, his varied service had meant that he had never quite got the hang of family life; and three tours with the SAS had burdened an already strained relationship which finally snapped when he had copped that bullet in the lung.

"I didn't know," he said.

Jenny didn't reply.

"I'm sorry."

"So was David."

Christ, but she knew how to twist the knife!

How had things become so poisoned? Where had it all gone sliding off the rails? Silly bloody question – it was the army, of course: that and his voluntary returns to a war zone when he could have had the cushy life in Germany.

"You really are a bastard, Peter. But then, what made me think you could've changed?"

With that, she finished her drink and rose and made her way into the car park. Fuming, Wilcox followed and a minute later they were speeding away through the dusk.

Marjory tried to persuade him to stay overnight, to drive back to London in the morning, but he declined. She was obviously disappointed but refrained from pressing him too far as the tension between himself and her daughter had become a tangible thing and would have upset David.

Before he left, Wilcox went upstairs to see his son. His bedroom was a shrine to Liverpool Football Club and the only free space was the window, though he had even once tried to cover that until his mother objected.

He was sleeping. Wilcox stood over him a while, noting how closely he resembled Jenny – they had the same almond-shaped eyes, delicate bones and fine fair hair – while the only thing he had inherited from his father was his smile.

He bent down and kissed him on the forehead. "So long, tiger," he said, then silently withdrew closing the door behind him.

"Take care of yourself, darling," Marjory said, giving him a hug.

"I will; and you take care of Tom."

"How could I break the habit of a lifetime?"

"Listen to her," Tom replied mischievously. "Anyone'd think it was all cakes and ale!"

Then Jenny followed him out into the night and walked with him to his car. She was still cross, but there was a noticeable softening in her demeanour. He unlocked the door and turned to face her. In the pale glow of the moonlight, her fragile beauty made her look like a doll. For a while they stood in silence; then he bent and kissed her on the cheek.

"I'll see you in a month," he said. "Or sooner, if I may?"

"You may."

"I love you, Jen."

"I know you do."

He reached down and held her, then kissed her again and slid behind the wheel of his car.

"But you're still a bastard," she added with a smile.

He grinned and, turning the engine over, waved goodbye and thrummed off down the road.

CHAPTER 2

THEY met on the top floor of a multi-storey car park in the City Centre. Donal Brady had never seen the brummy corporal before and remarked at once the air of indolence which hung upon his flabby jowls. In appearance, he was a marathon from the ideal image of a soldier; his belly sagged and he carried himself in a way which seemed to suggest that his weight was an unfamiliar burden. Donal put his height at the average and his age at maybe thirty; but it was only when the corporal turned to close the door of his red Vauxhall Cavalier that he saw why the Council had codenamed him 'Monk': the top of his head was as bald as a Dominican Friar's.

Stepping from concealment behind a concrete pillar, Donal whistled softly. The soldier started, glancing nervously about him till he saw the balaclava'd figure, then wallowed across towards him, the perspiration on his face shining in the harsh strip-lighting.

"Finnegan ...?"

Donal nodded. "D'ye bring the stuff?"

"Did you bring the markers?"

Donal waved a small white envelope and the corporal reached into his jacket, withdrawing a buff-coloured folder. Making the exchange, Donal glanced quickly through the contents; there were five sheets in all, photostats with hazy mugshots and he was relieved to see that his was not among them. The corporal meanwhile had torn his envelope open and was thumbing with frantic disbelief through the gambling I.O.U.s.

"Wha's goin' on?" he demanded. "Where's the fookin' rest?"

"D'ye really think we'd let ye go with both your balls intact?"

"Bastard!"

It wasn't hard to avoid the attack. Donal merely stepped aside and watched as the ponderous soldier's weight carried him crashing to the ground. Stabilising on all-fours, the corporal's shoulders shook with rage and despair.

"You fookin' promised ... said it was quits!"

Like your people told me, Donal thought, feeling a mixture of pity and disgust.

"Get up."

The soldier obeyed. His eyes were brimming, but there was a flame of desperation which put Donal on his guard.

"Don't even think about drawin' your gun," he said. "There's a man behind that pillar an' another by the stairs."

It was a bluff, of course, but the corporal didn't know that. He hesitated and the light in his eyes grew dim.

"Back t'your car, now."

"What about my markers?"

"They'll be safe. Ye can bet on that."

As the soldier shuffled away, Donal slipped the folder into his jacket. There was a grotesque irony at work which he had not failed to appreciate: two fish caught on the hooks of betrayal, one reluctant, the other resigned; both at work for each other's masters; and one, by wriggling free, ensuring the landing of the other. He turned and walked across to the stairs, removing his balaclava and discarding it in a bin near the lifts. It was some bloody world when even an item of clothing could land you in a cell and, descending to the ground floor, he climbed into his car and drove away.

They had called the operation 'Gorgon', a joint-services initiative designed to infiltrate the Provisional IRA. Instead of putting a man in on the ground, it was decided to compromise someone already in place – a man with the ability and potential to climb the ladder to a position of trust – and Donal Brady had been that man.

In the security of his study he perused the scant information which the Intelligence corporal had given him. Fortunately there was very little of value which the Chief could sink his teeth into; but the fact remained that the handlers' dossiers could conceivably lead to their discovery. And if that happened – when that happened – Donal Brady's candle would be snuffed.

With eyes upon the hazy shot of the man he had known only as Zeus, but now as William Tyndall, he found his mind drifting back into the past.

Nine years ago, he and a couple of boys had been rigging explosives in a van beside a busy supermarket. Brigade Staff had said it was owned by the Brits and that they wanted an example made; but something had gone wrong: the next thing they had known they were surrounded by a unit of Paras. The lads had panicked, decided they would try and fight their way out, and before he had been able to stop them they had leapt into the open, guns blazing, to be cut down in a murderous crossfire. Anxious to avoid their fate, he had immediately offered his surrender; the soldiers had battered him black-and-blue and by nightfall he was banged-up in a cell in Castlereagh.

He had been told what to expect, but the knowing had only made it worse. He was stripped and beaten, left in the dark, beaten again, then dragged into a brightly-lit tiled room and subjected to the jet of a powerful hose until his testacles felt like they had been put through a wringer. Then he was hauled back to his cell, moaning with pain and shivering with cold and fear, left for a while, and then the whole damn thing had started again.

Time had lost all meaning and the minutes had seemed like hours. No blanket to keep him warm, he could not even rub his battered body to restore the circulation as the pain was too intense. Beyond the cell door, he had heard the screams for mercy as other prisoners rode the merry-go-round of brutality. He knew they were recordings, but they had sounded so immediate and real; and after another visit to the hose, he no longer knew anything but his pain.

And then the beatings had stopped. The cell door had opened and into the harsh glare of light he had seen the figure of a man stood in the doorway. Filled with fear, he hugged himself into the corner, tensed to withstand the flurry of fists and boots; but instead there came the cultured tones of a man who spoke so gently that, in spite of himself, he had relinquished what remained of his resistance.

First they had returned his clothes and given him a blanket for warmth; then he had been taken to a small furnished room where they had given him some coffee and a cigarette. Finally, the man who had delivered him from violence reappeared and the process of turning him into an informer had begun.

In return for his co-operation, he was promised release, reward and protection.

"An' if I refuse?" he had asked through cut and swollen lips.

"You go back to the beatings, then we'll turn you loose and put the word out that you've taken British gold."

And that's how they did it Donal thought bitterly as he stared at Tyndall's photograph. It didn't matter which way you jumped: either way you were fucked.

He replaced the papers in the file and sealed it in a large brown padded envelope. Then, switching off the anglepoise lamp on his desk, he crossed the hall to the living room where Moira and the kids were watching telly.

"See ye later."

"Where are ye goin'?"

"I'll be back in time for dinner," he replied.

Sweet Christ, how would they cope when they discovered he was a traitor? It was a though he had always kept pushed tight in the darkest corner of his mind and, as he let himself out into the rain and bitter cold, he shivered as he tried to imagine the consequences.

It was almost four o'clock when he reached Martin Kennedy's. A phone call on the way to let the Chief know he was coming, then a thirty-minute drive into the country. The rain had eased and the scent of the moist fields clung to the eddies of the breeze; huddling deeper in his waterproof jacket, he stood a moment savouring the tranquillity, then reluctantly set off up the woodland track to the farmhouse.

"Good t'see ye, Donal," the Chief said, answering the door. "C'mon in an' dry yoursel'; ye'll be catchin' your death o'cold."

A minute later he was steaming before the fire and Kennedy was examining the file.

"S'not very much," he said, withdrawing the five flimsy sheets. "Are ye sure he's not holdin' out on us?"

"He's a frightened man, Mister Kennedy."

"An' so he bloody should be," the Chief replied, sitting behind his desk.

Donal nodded: Monk wasn't the only one who was frightened; and it was all he could do to stay in the same room as the man who was hunting him.

Kennedy looked strangely innocuous with glasses, like a kindly old schoolteacher, and it was almost impossible to believe that he was what he was: a terrorist godfather. He was a legend in the Movement, renowned for his cruelty, cunning and commitment, and had risen to command on a tidal wave of political and sectarian murder which cast even the mad-dogs into the shade. Where other men wavered, Kennedy stood firm. Back in the seventies, he had single-handedly taken on a unit of Paras, killing two and forcing them into retreat. This act alone would have established him in the popular mythology; but it was only one deed among many in a long and bloody career – and now his credibility was being damaged.

Donal looked at the pictures on the mantle. There was a family shot posed while on holiday in Connemara, taken at the time Kennedy was making his name with the Belfast Brigade; one of a wee girl, Oona, his daughter, from whom he was estranged and who was now wed and living on a farm in Limerick; another of a smiling young man in bomber jacket, John-Jo, his son, now serving life in the Kesh for whacking a Proddy building-contractor; and finally in a silver frame in the foreground was a sepia shot of a sad but lovely-looking young woman, Mary Jean, his wife, who had died of cancer seven years ago. Whatever capacity for emotion, for softness, he had ever had died with her; and when she had gone he had intensified his commitment to the Cause, ensuring him notice and a willing-hand to the top. Of all the men in the

Movement, there were none so bloody chilling; and Donal felt the ice run up his spine as he considered his position.

"Five men runnin' the tout an' none of 'em from the regular channels," the Chief said at last. "Five men pulled off other things to concentrate only on him. Now, why d'ye suppose that was?"

Donal shrugged. "Maybe they were tired of all the fuck-ups?"

In the past, co-operation between the Intelligence departments of the security forces in Ulster was notoriously poor. Territorial jealousies undermined much of what they tried to achieve and, in the seventies, things had become dangerously tangled to the point of absurdity. No department was willing to share its information and sources, stumbling on and blowing the covers of men each had working on the ground, resulting in the capture and killing of informers and occasionally even handlers, and the abrupt cessation in the flow of valuable information.

For the Provos, of course, it had been like Christmas. They had made good use of the confusion, tightening their structure and reducing the margins for success of any future attempts at penetration. In view of the collapse in their operational integrity, the security forces had no choice but to overhaul their system; but this bolting-of-the-stable-door philosophy arrived too late for the men whose lives had been lost, and the new atmosphere in which the various Intelligence departments were to operate was poisoned with the bitterness of the past. But there was an improvement.

Kennedy nodded. "Sounds about right. They'd certainly want t'protect their bloody man. But it's an interestin' operation all the same." He turned again to the file and rapidly extracted nuggets of information. "William Tyndall, K Section, MI5; Major Alan Pennick, G1 Intelligence; Major Nigel Barrett, Signals Intelligence, Captain Peter Wilcox, SAS; an' our old pal Inspector Leahy, RUC Special Branch. Ye remember Leahy?"

Donal remembered. They had whacked him a year ago on the Newtownards to Ballycopeland Road, and he felt relieved one of the leads had gone.

"Intelligence men, an SAS contact an' a lifter. Theory's the same; but with 'em all bein' drawn together from different fields, it's a helluva lot stronger in the water."

"So, what comes next?" Donal asked, trying to keep the tremor from his voice.

"When's Reilly an' the new lads gonna be ready for the bloodin'?"

"Coupla weeks."

"Not good enough."

"A week on the outside."

"Ye'll have t'go an' hurry 'em along."

"I'll go tomorrow."

"Ye'll go tonight. An' when ye get back ye'll be takin' a trip t'London."

It was pointless arguing. Kennedy had it all worked out. But Donal had this nasty feeling that things were slipping away and there was nothing he could do about it.

"London?" he asked as Kennedy returned the papers to the file and locked them away inside his desk. "Why London?"

"Apart from the fact we need t'make arrangements for the arrival of Reilly's ASU, there's a wee lass in Whitehall who can save us a deal o'trouble by tellin' us where we can lay hands on our men."

A glimmer of hope ...?

"Right, well, I'd best be off, then."

"Call me when ye get back."

Donal headed gratefully for the door.

"An' Donal ...?"

"Mister Kennedy?"

"Ye've done well. It won't be forgotten."

Too bloody right it wouldn't! he thought as he hurried back out into the rain. Nine years of treachery, of living a lie, had finally caught up to him; and when he reached his car he was hardly in a fit state to drive.

CHAPTER 3

THE arms shipment arrived on Sunday night. Patrick Kelly, a small, lean, rat-faced man with lank ginger hair hauled open the doors of the warehouse and waved the truck inside.

"Jesus, Seamie, ye had the shit scared out o'me," he said as he closed and locked the door. "Ye were supposed t'be here two bloody hours ago!"

"Aye, well, I stopped off t' get a bite to eat," said the dark- haired man in the cab as he cut the engine.

"Ye're a cocky bastard."

"An' ye're an ugly one."

"I thought ye'd been picked up for sure."

Seamie jumped down and stretched. "Ye worry too much."

"An' you don't worry enough!"

Kelly dropped the tailgate and clambered into the trailer. Ten minutes later, all the crates had been unloaded and neatly stacked in the corner.

"Hand me that crowbar," Kelly said.

With a grunt he lifted the lid of one of the crates to expose half-a-dozen AK47 Russian assault rifles wrapped in greasy paper.

Seamie whistled. "Would ye look at that, now."

"Horrible bloody things," Kelly replied, replacing and securing the lid. He was a conduit – not a soldier – and hated coming into contact with the tools of violence.

He jemmied open a few more crates at random, revealing an assortment of handguns, fragmentation grenades and ammunition. The last crate he opened was packed with the Czechoslovakian-manufactured explosive Semtex and he almost gagged as the sickly scent of marzipan filled his nostrils.

"Shaaysuzz, will ye shut up that box!" he cried, backing away.

Seamie grinned. "Minds me o'them Easter cakes me Ma made when I was a kid."

Kelly cursed. Seamie hammered back the lid and returned the crate to the stack. Then they left by the side entrance where Kelly's silver BMW was parked.

"What now?" Seamie asked

"We 'phone the Man an' tell 'im it's arrived."

As they drove away they did not see the car start up behind them. Right at the gates and along the quiet road to the junction, it stayed well back and followed them to Ealing.

Harry Thomson, acting Director of 'K' Branch, MI5, was sitting in the easy chair in his sparsely furnished office overlooking Curzon Street. He was a nondescript man in his mid-forties, with greying hair combed neatly back from his lined forehead and temples and a passive, almost kindly face which suggested he could be entrusted with confidences.

Thomson had taken over when his predecessor, William Tyndall, had died and for three months he had occupied the Chair. But as yet there had been no sign that his promotion would be permanent. The DG had decided on a trial period to assess his suitability for the post and Thomson had long been accustomed to taking things as they came.

There was a knock on the door and a youthful face looked apprehensively round the office.

"Sir ...?"

"What is it, Jamie?"

"Oh. Message from Alpha, sir. The arms have arrived."

MI6 had tracked them from Libya along the Middle Eastern corridors to the port of Marseilles. As soon as they had entered the British three-mile limit on a Portugese freighter, responsibility had passed to MI5 as Six did not have the authority to operate domestically.

"Thank you, Jamie."

"Shall I notify Special Branch, Sir?"

"And have them clomping round disturbing the grouse? No. Maintain a watching brief. Find out who's involved. Then we can involve our Uncle Bill."

"Very good, Sir," the youth replied, closing the door softly behind him.

Jamie Daniels had been with the department for three months, having spent a year-and-a-half in Registry. A graduate from Magdalen College, Oxford, he was only twenty-five, and Thomson found his eagerness unsettling. My God, was I ever like that? he wondered. Probably; but it was all so long ago. He sighed and moved across to his desk where he resumed his perusal of the file which had been sent across from Century House earlier that day. Libyan arms for Irish terror: another campaign was on its way — but at least this time they were prepared.

Dusk. Three men cradling Armalites in the crooks of their elbows crawled through the undergrowth towards the barn. It had been raining and their camouflaged uniforms were sodden and stained with mud. Suddenly, a burst of automatic fire raked the ground before them.

Scrambling to their feet, they stumbled into one another as they raced in search of cover.

"What the hell was that?" Tim Reilly yelled from the barn doorway, an AK angled loosely across his chest. "Ye're makin' more noise than a man with an elephant standin' on his bollocks!"

They laughed nervously.

"Funny is it? Jus' you try laughin' when the bastard Brits blow that shit which passes for your brains out through the tops o'your stupid fuckin' heads!"

The laughter stopped.

"Right!" he continued. "Do it again, but this time do it properly 'cause I'll be aimin' low!"

The three youths exchanged a worried glance and grumbled as they slipped back down the slope.

A battered Cortina drove up the path and parked beside the barn. Donal Brady clambered out and saw Reilly pass a despairing hand across his cropped dark hair.

"Trouble?" he asked.

"These pricks couldn't crawl through a pile o'shit if ye threw 'em in it!" he said hopelessly. "Ye're a long way from Belfast, Donal. What're ye after?"

"We've a job for ye. Across the water."

"I've some whiskey in the house. We can talk there."

"What about them?" Donal asked, watching the men walking down the hill.

Reilly spat. "Fuck 'em. The exercise'll do 'em good."

"Jesus, are ye bloody mad?"

Donal had outlined Kennedy's plan to locate and snatch the Gorgon team.

"It's hard enough operatin' on the mainland as it is, never mind pullin' a crazy stunt like that!"

Reilly downed his whiskey fast, poured another and sat staring into its amber depths.

"Crazy or not, it has t'be done."

"By the end of the week an' with them!" Reilly replied, jerking a dismissive thumb at the three trainees standing by the barn smoking and playing with their rifles as if they were toys.

"Have ye a better idea?" Donal asked testily. "Cause if ye have I'm sure the Chief'd love t'hear it."

"Shit, Donal – what the fuck's been going' on? Since when d'we send lambs into the field? Christ, these lads have only had a couple o'weeks trainin' an' I'll tell ye now they'll be more of a hindrance than a help."

"I'm sorry, Tim, but that's the way it has t'be. Ye'll jus' have t'do your best t'get 'em operational."

"The impossible I can manage," Reilly said bitterly. "But miracles take a little longer."

Donal finished his drink and set the tumbler down beside the sink.

"Ye'll be contacted within the next few days. In the meantime push 'em as hard as ye bloody well can."

A parting nod and he was gone. Reilly shook his head. Then, pouring the whiskey back into the bottle and slamming in the stopper, he picked up his rifle and strode back out to the barn.

"Right, ye lazy shites! Move your arses back down that hill! An' this time if I see so much as a blade o'grass tremble, I'll shoot ye meself an' save the bloody Brits the trouble!"

It was almost midnight when Donal got back home. Pushing the front door softly closed, he turned to find Moira glaring down at him from the top of the stairs.

"Where the hell have you been?" she demanded. "Your bloody dinner burned to a crisp six hours ago!"

"I'm sorry."

Her response was the slamming of the bedroom door and Donal cursed. He had troubles enough on his mind without her adding to them. Going into his study, he slumped tiredly at his desk. He longed to sleep and it felt like there were grains of sand behind his lids which were trying to make pearls of his eyeballs.

"Jesus, for an end to this," he prayed, reaching for a copy of 'Classic Myth and Legend' by A.R. Hope-Moncrieff from his heavily-burdened bookshelves. The book had been a 'gift' from Tyndall. Whenever there was something to be communicated, they would select the appropriate words from the text, referring to them by page number, line number and the number of the word within the line. As a way of passing information, it was as old as God's green hills; but it was also virtually infallible since, if the title and edition of the book were unknown, the numbers could not be turned back into words.

Nine years of familiarity had given Donal a mastery of the task. He produced a rapid and concise account of Kennedy's plan to snatch his handlers, information regarding the despatch of Reilly's ASU and his own impending trip to London. Then, almost feverishly, he added a request for the immediate removal of himself and his family to a place of safety.

With that, he tore the sheet and the one immediately below it from the pad. The message he folded and stuffed into his pocket; the blank sheet scored with indentations, he tore into bits and burned in his ashtray. Only one more thing remained to be done: the delivery of the letter. He switched off the desk light and went back out into the hallway.

Silence. No light spilled from beneath the bedroom door; either Moira was asleep or she was trying to. He let himself out into the night and crossed the lawn to his car. A keen wind tore at his waterproof jacket but he hardly seemed to notice. A minute later he was keying the ignition and cursing as the engine refused to catch. He didn't see Moira watching him from the window and probably wouldn't have cared. Finally the car coughed into life and he shot off into the night. Moira watched him go, listening to the note of his engine growing faint until it faded altogether, then stepped back letting the curtain fall back into place, a look of puzzled concern upon her face.

The safest and most common method of communication between an agent and his handler was the letter-drop, and for the past three months Donal had been using a loose brick in the shell of a bombed-out building in the suburbs.

Half-an-hour after setting out from home, he was stumbling through the rubble to the drop. The footing was treacherous; twice he slipped, gashing his hand and tearing the right knee of his jeans. But finally, after much concentration and effort, he reached the drop-off point.

With his left hand he withdrew the loose brick; transferring it to his damaged right, he pulled the message from his pocket with an awkward gesture and stuffed it into the hole. Then he replaced the brick and scrambled back to the road.

For the sake of security, it was essential that the drop be disturbed only when a desposit had been made. This was determined by an agreed signal, a chalk mark on the lamp post at the corner. Donal hurried across, fishing a piece of red chalk from his jacket pocket and, as he stooped to make the mark, he saw a mark already there. That meant his handlers had left something for him. He quickly erased and replaced the mark, then clambered back across the rubble to the drop. Again he removed the brick and, this time, found the message which had been left for him. One glance sent a shiver down his spine. It wasn't in code.

Back home in his study, he tore the en claire message from his pocket and sat down behind his desk. There were only seven words, but they might have weighed a ton each for the effect they had upon him.

'URGENT MEET. USE CONTACT No. REPEAT URGENT.'

The contact number Tyndall had given him was only to be used in cases of emergency and Donal had never had occasion to use it before. Whatever it was that had happened it must have been something bloody serious and he reached a trembling hand towards the 'phone.

CHAPTER 4

MONDAY morning and the boys were back from a pricing-job in Wales. Mike Travis, a former sergeant in the Paras and as big and hard as they came, was perched on the edge of the desk as he made his report to Wilcox.

"Big place, lots of windows, cold as a barn and a doddle to enter. We gave 'em an estimate. Said they'd think about it, get back to us sometime in the week." He ran a broad hand across his shorn blond head. "But I wouldn't hold me breath. Bloody place is so rundown, they're obviously short on the readies. Might as well concentrate on that job in Bucks."

"D'you know the old bugger wanted a virtual freebie?" said Dizzy Greaves, the long-haired ex-marine.

Travis grinned. "On account of his having been a colonel, like."

"An' what did you say?" Jacko asked.

Dizzy chuckled. "Told him we only did 'specials' for Generals and above.

Wilcox turned to Charlie Kane, a gingery scouser who had recently been discharged from the SAS.

"What do you think, Charlie?" he asked.

"Same as the boys. We can only trim the cost so much, but we're not a friggin' charity."

"Then Bucks it is," said Wilcox, withdrawing a ledger from the safe beside the desk and scratching the Welsh job from the folio. "Mike, you and Charlie can take it. Dizzy can finish that wiring job in the Bush."

"Oh, ta very much!"

"But first we have a little job in Acton to take care of." He held up a copy of the local paper with the headline YOUTHS TERRORISE OLD FOLK ON ESTATE. "Jacko's idea – no profit but moral. But then, he always fancied being Robin Hood."

Above the ribald comments the ugly cockney explained it was a favour to his auntie who had friends upon the estate. She believed there was more to it than bored youths enlivening their days; and besides, it was a break from their routine.

There were four of them altogether, real scruff-uglies carrying baseball bats. The sixteenth floor of this tower block on the Grosvenor Estate in East Acton had been virtually cleared of its residents; apart from an Indian family and a young unmarried mother, there was an elderly couple named Bainbridge who had refused to 'take the hint' and it was before their flat that the persuaders had assembled.

They didn't see the two masked figures silently approaching from opposite ends of the walkway. As one of the uglies advanced to batter down the door, the tall figure to their left lobbed a cylindrical object down the drainage gully towards them. Moments later, there was a blinding flash and a deafening bang; and then, during the next few seconds while their senses were disabled, each was knocked to the floor by a series of punishing blows which felt like the building had collapsed on them.

The masked men had already picked out the leader, a pit-faced skinhead with a red feather earring. They hauled him to his feet and dragged him, whimpering, into the lift which a third masked man had held. As they descended, they hooded the prisoner and bound his wrists and ankles with gaffer tape; then they bundled him into the back of a Transit van which was waiting in the basement car park with its engine running.

Exactly three minutes seven seconds after the assault had begun, they were tooling away towards the Uxbridge Road. The inhabitants of the tower block gradually filtered from their homes in search of the source of the disturbance; but the sixteenth floor was as quiet as a tomb.

The last thing Detective Inspector Regis needed at ten o'clock on a Monday morning was the report of an explosion on his manor. Detective Constable Whyte turned into the Grosvenor and killed the engine and they watched as a group of dirty kids on bicycles tore recklessly through the wasteground that had once been the gardens.

The estate was just like any other seedy inner-city project; conceived in the sixties as a cost-effective and efficient way of housing the masses, the architect's dream had turned into a nightmare of dehumanising squalor and a breeding ground for every type of crime from drugs to murder. And Regis hated the bloody place.

"What's the bet the bloody lift's buggered?" he said as he clambered from the car.

Whyte grinned. "We can alway stop half-way if you get tired."

Regis gave him a withering look. The constable was tall, tanned, fit and fair, whereas he was short, pale, fat and balding. A horrible constrast when you came to think about it; but at least he had the benefit of rank.

"Fancy yourself back in uniform do you, son?" he asked.

Whyte didn't reply. Regis shoved his hands into his overcoat pockets and turned with a purposeful air to face the tower block.

"Come on, then. Let's get this bloody job over with."

The terrified skinhead sat tied to a wooden chair in the lock-up surrounded by five masked men.

"Let me see if I've got this straight," said the mask with the posh voice. "You were hired by someone in the Council to clear a few flats so he could knock them out to the squatters at a reduced rent and pocket the money?"

"Yeah!"

"What's his name?"

"What?"

"This man in the Council?"

"Who are ya?"

"Man asked you a question, toe rag."

Skinhead looked nervously at the man who had spoken, a giant regarding him over a splintered pick-axe handle.

"Ph-Phillips ... Fieldin' ..."

"Which?"

"Fieldin'!"

"And what was your cut in the action?"

"Fifty quid!"

"Per flat?"

"Yeah!"

"And how many flats have you cleared?"

"Shit, I don't ... Seven, eight ..."

The masks went into a huddle. While they talked, skinhead struggled against his bonds but quickly gave up when he found he was only making the rough knots bite deeper into his flesh.

"Right," continued posh voice, returning, "I want the names of everyone involved, beginning with your own. I want dates, locations, payoffs — the lot; and when you're done with that you're going to write it down and sign it."

"Fuck off!"

Posh voice nodded to the small mask beside him who produced a jerry can of petrol and doused the youth in the chair.

"Shit! You're fuckin' mad!"

"What's it going to be?" asked posh voice quietly.

"I can't! They'll fuckin' kill me!"

"I was 'opin' you'd say that," said small mask, spinning the wheel of his zippo. "Getcha jollies frightenin' grannies? Now it's your fuckin' turn, ya little shit! Step back, boys, we're gunner 'ave a barbie."

"NooOOO!"

As he stepped up with the flame flickering before him, a foul stench filled the air and skinhead slumped into a faint.

"Bloody 'ell! Wouldja believe it?"

"You telling me you'd keep your guts if someone threatened you with a Guy Fawkes job?" said giant mask, retreating.

"I ain't talkin' about the smell."

"Then what are you talking about?"

"Me bleedin' lighter's jus' run out."

"You evil little bastard!"

When skinhead came to, they freed his bonds and handed him a pen and pad; but he was trembling so violently that he was unable to write down what he told them, so posh voice relieved him of the burden and, gleaning further details, soon produced an upper-case account of the scam.

"Sign it," he commanded.

Skinhead shakily scrawled his name at the bottom of the page and posh voice recovered the pad.

"Right, hood him up and tie him."

"Whatcha gonna do wi' me?" asked skinhead, his muffled voice cracking into a whine.

"Do you know, that's a bloody good question," said giant mask when they had put him in the back of the Transit. "What *are* we going to do with him?"

"Oh, I'm sure we'll think of something," said Wilcox, removing his balaclava and sliding behind the driving wheel; and a moment later they were tooling away in the sunshine.

Two bloody hours they had been knocking on doors, trying to find out what had caused the bang. Regis's legs were killing him: the local brats, knowing they were busies, had sent both lifts to the basement, jamming the doors open with sticks and crushed beer cans, forcing them to use the stairs. That was bad enough. But what had really cooked his spleen was that no bugger seemed to know a thing!

"Marvellous, innit?" he said sourly as they finally hit the ground. "Seventeen floors with seven flats on each, walls like bloody rice paper and all they can whistle is Dixie!"

"Reckon it was just kids, myself," said Whyte. "Y'know, messing about with bangers."

"Dynamite'd be more up their street. 'Ere, what's goin' on over there?"

The lads on bicycles they had seen earlier in the day were gathered, pointing and jeering, around their motor.

"Oy! Clear off out of it!" cried Whyte, breaking into a run.

The kids scattered revealing the gaudily spray-canned logo 'Police' which ran the full length of the bodywork. Whyte came to a hesitant stop, then called back over his shoulder.

"Sir, I think you'd better come and have a look at this."

"I can bloody well see it!" Regis snapped. He could already hear the laughter back at the nick.

"Er, no sir ... this ..."

Whyte stepped aside and pointed to something writhing upon the back seat. Regis bent and stared through the window.

"Jesus bloody Christ!"

The two policemen stared in stunned disbelief at the skinhead who was gagged and trussed like a rodeo calf, with a sheet of folded paper taped to his forehead on which was written the words:

'DEAR OFFICER, I HAVE BEEN A NAUGHTY BOY.'

CHAPTER 5

SEAMIE pulled in before a detached red-brick house in Gordon Road, Ealing Broadway.

"There ye go, Mister Brady. Key's in the pot beside the door. Pat said ye're t'make yourself at home."

"Ye're not comin' in?"

"Nah, I've t'get back t'work."

Donal jumped out and pulled his suitcase from the boot. Seamie dropped the window.

"There's grub in the fridge an' booze in the lounge. Pat'll be in t'see ye sometime after six. Okay?"

Donal nodded.

"Right," Seamie continued, grinding into gear, "I'll be seein' ye."

He shot off down the road and Donal crossed the path to the house.

Key in the pot. Christ, with security like that it was small bloody wonder so many players were lifted! Half these bastards thought the Brits were soft in the head and it was thinking like that which set them on the path to the bridey. Pondering their stupidity as he stooped to fish out the key, he did not see the twitching net in the window of the house directly opposite. Nor did he know that he was trapped on film to be processed for ident by a team from MI5. Straightening, he keyed himself in and shut the door softly behind him.

"Donal Brady, born West Belfast, 1957," read Jamie Daniels from the file. "Suspected to have been involved in numerous bombings and sectarian shootings, but nothing was ever proved. It's believed he commanded a Provo Brigade for a year or two and then he dropped out of sight. The last entry's in ... early '84."

Harry Thomson, staring at the black-and-white glossies spread before him, grunted.

"Suspected – believed – that's not much bloody use, is it?"

"I'm afraid that's all we've got, sir. But I can contact G1 Intelligence, Lisburn, if you like and see if they've any more?"

"Do it now. Things are mysterious enough as it is without this pimpernel squirting more ink into the water."

Daniels withdrew. Thomson leant back into his chair with a sigh. A known terrorist whose record came to an abrupt stop nearly a decade ago suggested that some slack bugger had fallen down on the job. He stacked the photos and returned them to the file, then filled and lit his pipe. Jigsaws, jigsaws, disparate pieces, fragments of a picture which could only be surmised.

It was raining. Martin Kennedy was standing by the living room window watching the water run down the pane to collect in a shallow pool beneath the sill. There had been another ambush. Five men had been delivering crated weapons across the border in a lorry when they had been forced off the road by a unit of Paras and into a field. Two dead; three captured. A valuable shipment confiscated and another blow to his prestige.

One bad apple in a barrel of seven. One wee bastard fucking the life out of the Movement.

But who ...?

In a rare display of temper he spun and hurled his tumbler of whiskey into the fireplace where it smashed, the flames consuming the spirit with a satisfied roar.

Whoever the bastard tout was he was going to fucking pay. No quick hooding and a head-job on some wasteground, but a slow and painful death.

Back in the seventies when they had found a squealer in the East Tyrone Brigade, Kennedy had worked on the bastard with a tool box and a talent he had laboured to refine. Three days the little shite had lingered; three long days until the life was punished from him. Then they had strung him from a lamp post with a placard round his neck to serve as a warning to anyone else who was considering — or engaged in — the act of betrayal.

He fixed himself another drink and returned to the window. Yes, he would make the bastard pay; but first he had to find him.

And time was running out ...

Donal Brady stepped from the shower and rubbed himself vigorously dry. He shaved, dressed, then went back down into the kitchen where he fixed himself a cheese and ham salad sandwich and a cup of strong black coffee. Racing from Doncaster ... a programme for kiddies hosted by some balding, condescending twat ... a lousy Aussie soap where the sets had more animation than the actors ... and an old black-and-white starring Jimmy Stewart as a gentle man companioned by an invisible six-foot rabbit named Harvey. Deciding that would do, he plumped down into a deep-cushioned armchair and surrendered to the story.

At three forty-five, the credits rolled. Donal rose and switched off the set, then took the plate and mug into the kitchen where he dumped them in the sink. Sunshine poured in through the polished kitchen window. Deciding to go out for a walk, he grabbed his coat from the bannister rail and wandered out, dropping the door key back into the orange clay pot. In the house opposite, a short fair-haired man made a note of the time of his departure, while another man with dark hair left quietly in pursuit.

Christ, she was a tart, but Patrick Kelly liked them that way. As he pulled on his trousers, he could see her in the dressing table mirror, starkers but for a pair of laddered black stockings and her plump legs splayed like she had been staked out in the desert. Kelly's philosophy was crude but simple; always go for the dogs. No one else wanted them which meant that they were hungry for sex; and who the hell looked at the mantlepiece when poking the fire, anyway?

"You'll be back to finish the wall tomorrow?" she asked.

"I've another job in the mornin', but it shouldn't take too long."

"I'll expect you for lunch, then? One o'clock?"

"I'll be here."

"You'd better be."

He gave her the grin he thought displayed his rogueish Irish charm, then went downstairs where he preened in the hallway mirror before letting himself out into the street. The sun was blazing and he turned his happy face into the warm breeze. Christ, but it was grand to be alive! he thought as he jumped behind the wheel of his BMW; and as he drove away he did not see the red Fiesta follow.

Kennedy and the whole bloody mess seemed so damned far away to Donal as he sat on a bench on Haven Green devouring a cornetto. A group of boys played lazy football, while all around were people strolling, taking advantage of the weather.

It was like another world, here. No soldiers patrolling the streets, no armoured cars or armed police. No wonder so many of his countrymen came here to work and live. My God, if he could just disappear, vanish and leave it all behind him. He could send for Moira and the kids; they could start a new life, perhaps a business, and then ...

Suddenly, reality appeared and knocked his dreams aside. He was a tout — a traitor in the eyes and hearts of his people — what sort of a future did he have, could he offer his poor bloody family? Christ, he would be lucky if he still had a family when they found out what he was, what he had done. A bleak despair took hold of him as he considered what the future had in store.

The previous night, when he had found the en claire message at the drop, he had used the contact number Tyndall had given him. A woman had answered; he had told her why he was calling, but she had explained that his contact was at present unavailable and suggested that he call back in the morning. In a rage he had slammed down the receiver. Urgent it had said! Urgent and she could not even raise the bastard, whoever the hell he was! And then, the following morning — this morning — he had been roused at seven by one of Kennedy's stooges bearing a plane ticket for Ringway Airport, Manchester. Why bloody Manchester? The Chief had thought it safer that he take the train into London!

The way events had shaped he had been unable to reach his contact. The stooge had taken him to the airport and had stayed with him until his flight was called and he had joined the queue at the departure gate. 'Phoning from England was a possibility he had considered, but discarded since he would not be there very long. He had to put everything out of his mind but the tasks he had been charged to perform: first, to get some information on the present whereabouts of the men who had compromised and run him; second, to arrange with Patrick Kelly for the billeting of Tim Reilly's ASU; and finally, to give the information on the Gorgon team to Reilly who would then begin the operation to lift and interrogate them. That was when the clock began to tick, when his life was up for grabs; that was when the nightmare and the lies would come to an end, when the running began and the price of survival was the destruction of all he had known.

"Mister ...? 'Ey, Mister ...!"

He looked up and saw a young lad pointing to a football at rest a few feet from the bench. Rising, he kicked it back and watched the game restart; then, he wandered back to Gordon Road, the man from MI5 who had been sitting nearby walking after him.

At five-past six, Kelly arrived.

"Mother o'God, I didn't believe it when they said you was comin'!"

"Been a long time, Pat."

"Too bloody long!"

They laughed, shook hands, then Kelly cracked open a bottle of Bushmills.

"Now s'pose ye tell me why ye're here."

Donal told him Reilly's ASU needed settling.

"No problem, I've three places ye can choose from. But sure, ye didn't need t'come all this way for that."

"The Chief says ye've a line into the MOD."

"There was a wee lass I was shaggin' works there, aye; but I haven't seen her for a while."

"Well, I hope ye left her smilin'."

Kelly lowered his glass. "All right, Donal, why don't ye tell me what ye're after."

"We've a few names needin' addressed. Military men possibly retired."

"Ye don't want much!"

"Can ye do it?"

Troubled, Kelly sat in the armchair by the window. "I don't know. Like I said, I've not seen her for a while. Christ, I can remember when it was only the bullet or the ballot-box – no one said anythin' about the bed bein' part o'the equation!"

"War's hell," Donal said.

Kelly grinned. "Ain't that the truth! Last time she took half the skin off me back – t'was a week before I dared have it off again!" He finished his drink and ran the back of his hand across his thin mouth. "What was it your man said? T'is a far, far better thing I do, than I have ever done? I'll give her a bell this evenin'; but there's no guarantee I'll come up with the goods." He rose and refilled their glasses. "Christ, the things we do for Ireland!"

Harry Thomson read with a growing disbelief the file which Jamie Daniels had handed to him. William Tyndall, his former chief, had been running an agent in Ulster long after he had earned his promotion to a desk job back in London. What the hell had he been playing at?

"Why have I not heard of this before?" he demanded.

"I'm afraid we didn't know," Daniels replied nervously. "It seems he was charged with setting up a compromise-and-turn job when the system in Ulster fell to pieces. He should have handed over when he came back here, you know, to G1 Intelligence, but he didn't, and they're hopping bloody mad about it since the info he supplied was first-rate.

All Thomson needed at this fragile stage in his career was a dead man's foul-up landing in his lap. Still, he could always throw it back.

"Ring Colonel Harris in Lisburn. Tell him to pick up the strings and run this Perseus himself."

"That's just it, sir. He can't."

"What do you mean he can't?"

"No one seems to know who he is."

"What?"

"From what I can gather, Mister Tyndall was the only member of the team who knew the man. Apparently, he felt it would be safer that way. You know, less chance of a leak."

Oh, this just got better and better!

"How was he getting his information?" Thomson asked. "What was the set-up?"

"One of our lads kept an eye on the drop. Whenever something turned up he'd collect it and send it here."

"Which means Tyndall dismantled the original com-line, returning his men to their units?"

"That's about the size of it, sir, yes."

"Bit of a bloody cock up."

"I-I'm afraid that's not all, sir."

"You mean there's more?"

"Yes, sir. When Mister Tyndall passed away, our man left an urgent message at the drop asking Perseus to get in touch, you know, to use the emergency number. Well, it seems the message sat there undisturbed for three months and when Perseus finally telephoned him he was out on a job with RUC Special Branch and missed the call."

"I'm sure he'll ring again."

"Yes, sir. But ..."

"Go on," Thomson replied with a weary sigh.

"Well, sir, our man went back to the drop this morning to leave a list of times when he could be reached and found a coded message, quite a long one I believe."

"And what did it say?"

Daniels didn't reply.

"Well?"

"We — that is he — doesn't know ..."

"He doesn't know?"

"No, sir."

"And why doesn't he know?"

"He can't decode it. He doesn't have the key."

"So, what you're telling me," said Thomson, keeping his patience with difficulty, "is that we have a man in on the ground, that we don't know who he is and that we can't decode his message. Is that what you're saying?"

Daniels shuffled uncomfortably. "Yes, sir — I think that pretty well sums it up."

"And they call our profession 'Intelligence'! Right, I think you'd better recall 'our man' to answer some questions. Then you can collate a file regarding all information passed by this Perseus character to the security forces in Northern Ireland so we can build up a picture. Then you can take the latest message down the hall to Bob Eyre and see if he can't crack the bloody thing. And when you've seen to all of that you can pay a visit to Registry and pull the files on the Gorgon team. I want them located and I want them questioned. In every operation you pick up scraps which don't directly concern you and there's always the chance that one of them knows who the bugger is."

"Yes, sir."

Daniels headed gratefully for the door.

"And Jamie ...?"

"Sir?"

"Donal Brady. Have you managed to fill in the gaps?"

"I'm afraid not, sir. Lisburn came up dry."

"I wonder why that doesn't surprise me," Thomson said, waving him away.

He rose and moved to the bureau in the corner where he poured himself a scotch. What with an IRA arms shipment which suggested yet another mainland campaign, a terrorist whose past had simply melted into thin air, and an agent who was so secret that not even his masters knew who he was, it was turning into one hell of a week ... and it wasn't even Tuesday.

CHAPTER 6

THE bomb in the shopping centre exploded at precisely half-past ten. The telephoned warning had come too late and the emergency services arrived to find the scattered and dismembered bodies of women and children lying on frosted mattresses of broken glass. Each shop front had been blown in – the goods displayed in the large-framed windows were charred and speared on jagged shards, and the paved pedestrian area was littered with rubble and resounded with the distressed cries of the injured.

As police cordoned off the area, television news teams leapt from their vans and started filming this latest atrocity in the Province. Detective Chief Inspector Rogan of the RUC was speaking to a knot of blackened firemen when Jill Davis from the BBC approached with a microphone in her hand.

"Chief Inspector. Could you tell us what happened?"

Rogan looked at the camera with distaste. "That's just what we're tryin' to ascertain. Now, if you'll excuse – "

"But you will confirm it was a bomb?" she persisted.

"Of course it was a f--. Yes, it was a bomb."

"Terrorist operations in the Province have been noticeably curtailed. Do you think this is a message to the security forces?"

"I think this is a message to the people of Ulster."

"Could you be more specific?"

"As long as these murderers are shielded by certain sections of the community, the violence will continue."

"So in effect what you're saying is that the people who are protecting the terrorists are just as guilty as those who planted the bomb?"

"That's what I'm sayin'."

"Chief Inspector, thank you."

Rogan nodded and returned to the firemen. The reporter turned to the camera.

"Another bomb explodes in Ulster and the violence continues. The casualty rate is tallied at nineteen, with six fatalities and more expected to follow before the end of the day. Although no one has yet come forward to claim responsibility, it is believed to be the work of the Provisional IRA. This is Jill Davis for the BBC in Belfast."

Finbar Sullivan paid the taxi driver and keyed himself into his house. He took off his jacket and, as he turned to hang it up on the stand beside the door, saw one of the men standing in the front room doorway.

"Where's Bridget?" Sullivan asked.

The man nodded behind him and Sullivan pushed past to find his wife sitting tensely on the sofa. She had been crying.

"Don't worry, Mister Sullivan. She's all right. Why don't ye make yourself a cuppa? Ye look like ye could use one."

Sullivan kneeled and took her hand. "Y'okay?" he asked and when she nodded, reached up and brushed away a stray strand of greying hair from her forehead. "I'm sorry," he whispered. "I'm so sorry ..."

Finbar Sullivan was employed as a warehouseman/driver by a British supermarket chain. The night before, as he and Bridget were getting ready for bed, the doorbell had rung and he had gone downstairs to find two strangers on the step.

"Finbar Sullivan?" they had asked; and when he nodded, one of them had produced a gun. "Irish Republican Army."

They had forced their way inside and Bridget, who had heard the commotion and come down to investigate, had seen the fear on her husband's face and the strangers with a weapon and had screamed. They had told her to shut up, then asked if they were alone in the house and had then driven them into the front room where they told Sullivan that they wanted him to do a job for them.

He was to leave the warehouse as usual and drive to a lock-up garage placed along his route where he would be met by three men with a packing crate which they would place inside the van. Then he was to carry out his delivery as normal; but instead of driving back to the warehouse he was to leave the van parked near the front of the supermarket and then make his way home by taxi.

To ensure that he complied with their instructions they had said that they were going to keep Bridget company, and Sullivan was left in no doubt as to the outcome of any failure on his part to carry out their demands.

"Ye did a good job, Mister Sullivan," said the man in the doorway. "But remember — not a word to anyone. Not if ye know what's good for ye ..."

As he spoke he removed a bullet from his jacket pocket and placed it on the coffee table. A moment later they were gone and Sullivan, screwing his eyes tight shut and dropping his head on Bridget's lap, wept and began to prepare a sanitised account for the police when they arrived.

Martin Kennedy was furious.

"What the fuckin' hell went wrong?"

"Everythin' was goin' accordin' t'plan," said Michael Donovan; "but when they went t'call it in they found the bloody box was vandalised. That's why there was a delay. It was an accident. There was nothin' they could do."

"That'll look grand on the press statement," said Christy Keegan.

"Then we'll issue a denial – disown the bloody thing!"

"An' who the hell's gonna believe that?"

Donovan thumped the table in defeated fury and slumped back in his chair.

The way things had been going it was the last thing they needed. Each man knew how much such fuck-ups damaged the standing of the Movement and they also knew that their positions as members of the Army Council meant that the buck stopped with them. Of course, the press would feed on it like vultures – mothers and children murdered while they shopped; it was also a godsend to the Brits who would use it to justify their continuing presence in Ulster, and the backlash would almost certainly affect the money which flowed into their coffers from the States.

"Why don't we blame it on the security forces?" suggested Patrick Wheelan. "Issue a statement sayin' they was given ample warnin', that it could've been avoided if they hadn't been so tardy respondin' t'the call."

"T'would never wash," said Eoin McCann. "The calls're logged. An' anyway, t'wasn't them who planted the bomb. The moral ground belongs t'them. We've helped them an' we've hurt ourselves."

"The way I see it," said Dermot O'Shea, "we've three options. One, we can deny it – but like Christy said, who'd believe us? Two, we can admit it, layin' ourselves open to all the criticism that would entail. An' three, we can simply keep our mouths shut, say nothin', ride it out until it slips away into memory."

"I don't see that it matters a shite what we do," said Tom Gallagher. "It happened – we can't bring back the dead – I mean, we're fightin' a war for fuck's sake – the innocent are bound t'suffer."

Donovan agreed with the crippled veteran beside him, but O'Shea did not.

"Jesus Christ, have ye not seen the news? Eight people dead an' some wee girl with her legs blown off at the knees!"

"Gettin' squeamish?" Donovan asked, his pocked face splitting into an evil smile.

"Jesus, ye're a fuckin' animal!"

"That's enough!" said Kennedy. "It's bad enough without us fightin' each other."

The two protagonists glared at other across the table and the Chief allowed a moment to pass before continuing.

"Like Dermot said, we've three options: denial, admission or silence. What's it gonna be?"

"We can forget denial for a start," said Keegan. "Everyone knows it was us an' denyin' it can only hurt us more."

"As will silence," said McCann. "Reports of what took place today'll be on every TV screen in the world. It doesn't matter how just is our cause, the images o'dead women an' children'll push the struggle aside, an' if we say nothin' we'll be seen as callous killers, nothin' more, an' we'll lose support."

"So it's admission, then?" asked Kennedy, searching the faces before him. "It's the only feasible option," said Keegan.

"Which raises the problem o'how we justify the slaughter of innocents," added O'Shea, knowing full well that they couldn't but recalling how past mistakes had been explained away by the Irish Republican Publicity Bureau.

"It occurs t'me," said Gallagher, "that we're goin' about this all wrong."

"What d'ye mean, Tom?" Kennedy asked.

"We're sittin' here discussin' an apology, we're bein' too defensive. Okay, so we fucked up. It happens, but there's nothin' we can do about it. We should be thinkin' o'somethin' bigger than what happened today, somethin' that'll knock this clean aside."

O'Shea could not believe what he was hearing and flung his hands into the air.

"Oh, that's fuckin' brilliant!" he cried. "Bury a slaughter beneath more killin'!"

"I'm talkin' a legitimate target that'll put us back on track. If we mount an op against the Brits—"

"With what? Christ, our operational strength's been damn near halved in the past six months! We've lost men dead, we've lost material an' credibility, an' because of today's bloody fiasco we're gonna lose support as well!"

"Dermot's right," said McCann. "It's best we keep a low profile. If we wait for everythin' t'settle down, it'll give us time t'think, t'see how things stand."

Gallagher lapsed into a sullen silence and Kennedy climbed to his feet.

"Christy, draft a statement for the press – somethin' along the lines that, while acceptin' full responsibility, we regret the loss of civilian lives, but that such losses are inevitable in war." Keegan nodded. Kennedy turned to Donovan. "An' Michael, get hold o'the boys who done it. Question 'em thoroughly an give me a detailed report by mornin'."

"D'ye, want 'em punished?"

Kennedy shook his head. "T'would serve no useful purpose. An' anyway, morale's low enough as it is."

The members of the Army council filed towards the door.

"Remember, now, after today they'll be thirsty for blood," Kennedy warned. "Keep your heads down, steer clear o'the clubs. An' for God's sake let's have no more fuckin' balls-ups!"

When they had gone, Kennedy's thoughts turned once again to the tout. Had one of these men whom he had trusted betrayed him, sold himself, his honour and his country and the Movement which was pledged to freeing it from colonial tyranny?

In a few days' time, God willing, the answer and the identity of the man would be known; and then, when he had been made to pay for his betrayal, the repair-work could begin.

CHAPTER 7

EMILY Baker watched the dawn break through a gap in the curtains. She hadn't slept well and her eyes felt grainy as if the Sandman of her childhood had tripped and given her a seven-night dusting instead of one. The digital clock on the bedside table read 5:43 and the alarm was set for 6:00. Reaching across gently so as not to disturb the figure slumbering beside her, she flicked the switch into the off position and, leaning back against the headboard, thought again on what had passed the night before when Patrick Kelly had telephoned and asked if he could see her.

Her first reaction had been to tell him a categorical no. It was almost five months since she had seen him last; he had promised he would call her, but of course he never had, and over the following weeks she had succumbed to such feelings of hurt and self-disgust that she had vowed never to let a man use her like that again. But there had been something in his voice which told her he was hurting, that he needed her; and before she realised what she was doing she had invited him round.

At first sight Emily was not very attractive. She had thin brown hair which she habitually wore in a bun, large ears and muddy brown eyes set in a face which seemed somehow unfinished as if the artist had been called away returning to discover that it had set with all its imperfections. Her body, too, seemed crudely fashioned: shoulders too broad, breasts too small; her legs, however, were shapely and long, but the effect was marred by the size of her feet — 'like something off a drayhorse' was but one of many hurtful comments made in her more vulnerable years.

With all her physical shortfalls she had never known what it was to be loved. Men would let their eyes slide past her, never resting on her like they did on other women, blonde, busty, coy and alluring women, the kind she had so desperately wanted to be. She knew what they called her type: dogs, bag-jobs, sympathy-fucks and Wednesday nighters'. But in spite of this her needs were real and her feelings she had learned to hold in abeyance. Sometimes. There were days when she longed to be held, to have someone look into her eyes and see the real her. But that was only a dream, a foolish longing — she knew that — and then she had met Patrick Kelly.

Dining alone one lunchtime she had seen the smiling Irishman at a a table in the corner with his friends. They were all dressed in denim, covered in brick-dust and Lord only knew what else and when their eyes had met she had hastily turned away. Next thing she remembered, he had ambled over and introduced himself. He had the bluest eyes she had ever seen and though his face was rather fox-like, he was attractive enough after a fashion and by the end of her lunch hour she had agreed to meet him that evening for a drink.

Over the following weeks she was bombarded with chocolates and flowers. He sent her cards, little notes — the sort of things she had heard about but had never before experienced. It made her feel wanted, young — not that she was old, though thirty- seven was way over the hill by some people's standards — and soon their relationship had broadened into the sexual.

That was when the whole thing had unravelled. The flowers, gifts and notes of endearment had given way to stand-ups, late arrivals and hurried knicker-tearing romps which usually ended with him racing off to keep another appointment. She had often wondered what had happened to change the way things had been. Was it her? Was it something she had said, or done? Patrick Kelly was the only man whom she had ever loved and she simply hadn't wanted to face the possibility that he had got what he was after and had consequently lost all interest in her. And then he had stopped coming to see her at all.

The first week had been the hardest. Coming home from work she would throw something in the oven and spend the evening picking at it in front of the telly. Often she cried, bitter tears of regret and self-recrimination. What had she done to drive him away? Why did he no longer want her? She wondered whether he was married — surely that would explain his staying away, his behaviour? But then she had stopped looking for reasons why he had chosen to drop her and instead tried to reconcile herself to the fact their relationship was dead. Time passed and the wound had begun to heal — but now he had come back into her life.

He seemed so different, altered somehow. He still looked the same, but there was a sadness about him which had not been there before. Over drinks they had made small-talk, catching up on each other's news and recalling some of the good times they had shared; and then he had begun to cry, a thing for which she had been totally unprepared.

It seemed that Kelly had spent the last few weeks in Belfast. What had been planned as an enjoyable family visit had turned into a nightmare when his younger brother, Danny, had been lifted under the Prevention of Terrorism Act and his mother had collapsed under the strain.

"I didn't know who else t'turn to," he had said, and all of Emily's bitterness had melted away and she had taken him in her arms to give him comfort.

Over coffee, Kelly had allowed himself to recover; then, he had unburdened himself in full.

"She's always had a weak heart, me Ma. First there was me Da passin' on last year; then me Auntie Mary got killed by some joyriders in Andytown; an' now this trouble with Danny. I'm scared she won't recover. They're tryin' t'say he's in the IRA. I mean, Christ, he's no more a terrorist than I am!"

"Surely they'll realise that and let him go?"

"Oh, girl, ye've no idea. Once the charge's levelled, the result's a foregone conclusion."

"But the jury—"

"It's a Diplock Court."

"I don't understand."

"There won't be a jury – just a judge. Juries can be tampered with, so they don't use 'em. It's supposed t'maintain the integrity o'the proceedin's. But it doesn't. The innocent go down 'longside the guilty. That's the way it is in Ulster. Danny hasn't got a bloody chance."

"There must be something you can do, someone you can talk to?"

"Only those who planned the lift, but the authorities are reluctant t'co-operate."

"What about your solicitor? Can't he persuade them?"

"He's tried, but they only keep fobbin' him off. All we have are some names, y'know, people who might be able t'help."

"So call them when the case comes up to trial."

"We don't know where they are, how t'get in touch with 'em."

"Surely the court could subpoena their attendance?"

"An' why should it bother? Danny's just another boggy."

She had sensed the bitterness which underlined the words and found it hard to believe such things could happen.

"An' anyway," he had continued, "they've probably already been reassigned."

"Can they do that?"

"Girl, they can do anythin' they like! It's them who make the rules; the rest of us just have t'live by 'em. The only way we can help Danny now, to see that justice is done, is t'find out where t'get hold o'the people who can help. But how the hell are we gonna do that ...?"

With that sentence lingering in the air, Kelly had taken hold of her hands and gently pressed his lips to them. Emily had felt the familiar thrill and, looking deep into his sad blue eyes, had felt herself grow angry at the injustice of it all.

"Let me help," she had whispered.

"Ye've already helped jus' by listenin', he had replied.
"No, I mean really help."
"What d'ye mean?"
"I could find these men for you."
The thought had obviously never entered Kelly's mind. "By Christ, I bet ye could at that!" For the first time that night he had really smiled. "God, Emily, I've been a fool. Can ye forgive me?"
"I can try."
"Ye're a helluva girl, Emily Baker," he had said, gathering her in his arms; "an' a man could do a lot worse!"
Then they had gone straight upstairs to bed where they had made love into the small hours.
At six o'clock she rolled back the covers and swung her feet to the floor. Kelly stirred.
"Good mornin'," she said.
"Already ...? Why don't ye come on back for a cuddle?"
"I can't. I've got to get ready for work."
"Ten minutes won't make ye late." He chuckled. "C'mon, I promise I'll go easy on ye."
She hesitated, then smiled. "All right. But no longer."
"Ye have my word."
When they were done and she had gone into the bathroom, Kelly stretched lazily and grinned. Whoever said you couldn't mix business with pleasure was wrong, he thought, then clambered out of bed to hunt for his clothes.
An hour later he keyed himself into the house in Gordon Road. He heard the sound of cutlery on china and breezed into the kitchen to find Donal Brady tucking into a fry-up.
"How's about ye, Donal?" he said, sliding into place on the bench beside him. "Jayz, but I've an appetite. D'ye mind?"
"Help yourself."
"Ta." He whipped a rasher and clothed it in a slice of fried bread. "Helluva night!"
"I hope ye got more'n a smile on your face?"
"Will have by tonight," he replied, spitting crumbs and raising a hand to wipe the grease from his chin. "Ah, man, it was beautiful! I had the silly tart eatin' right out o'me hand. I didn't even have to ask. She begged me t'let her help!"
Laughing as he chewed he bragged about the non-existent brother ploy he had used in order to gain her sympathy.
"An' if she checks?" Donal asked. "What then?"
"Did I not jus' tell ye she swallowed every bloody word? Honest, boy, ye should o'seen it — I was brilliant!"

"Ye always were a modest bastard," Donal said, rising and tightening the cord of his robe. "I'll see ye later."

"Where ye goin'?"

"I'm away t'have a shower."

"Are ye not gonna finish your breakfast?"

Donal shook his head. "I never did like too much grease."

His ambiguous response was lost on Kelly who was already tucking in. When he came back down an hour later, Kelly was gone and the unwashed plate lay greasy in the bowl. Cursing, Donal scrubbed it clean and placed it on the drainer. Kelly may have been a slut in every sense of the word, but he always came up with the goods.

Making a coffee, Donal went into the living room where he switched the TV on. The news was dominated by yesterday's blast and according to the report the Provisionals had claimed responsibility. During the night, the death toll had risen to ten and three of them were children. Turning it off, he shook his head at the waste and futility of it all.

Only a few more days, he thought, and for him it would all be over; a few more days and he would leave the whole bloody mess behind.

CHAPTER 8

OLD Mrs. Mawdsley found it hard to hide her disappointment. She thought it would have been far more exciting, but all the men from the Government seemed to do was sit there looking bored. Five days had passed since that nice Mr. Thomson called round to ask if he could borrow her front bedroom for a few days. He had shown her his warrant card, explaining that it was a matter of National Security; and Ethel and her husband, Tom, a veteran of Bomber Command, who were always ready to 'do their bit', had readily agreed.

Despite the initial thrill of being chosen to participate in a job of such importance, they had watched in consternation as three men had cleared a space around the window, pushing the double-bed against the back wall and moving the dressing-table out on to the landing.

"Oh, dear!" she had said. "You're not going to damage anything, are you?"

"Don't you worry," said the one who had called himself Smith. "We've done this kind of thing before and we've never broken a thing."

Although she had nodded gratefully, she had hardly felt reassured.

Then Smith had asked if he could take a look around the back of the house and Tom guided him away. While he was gone, the other two men had busied themselves before the window setting up cameras, complicated looking things on tripods with long lenses and dangly bits.

When Smith had returned he had asked what they knew about the man who owned the house across the road.

"Not a thing, I'm afraid," Tom had replied. "You know how it is these days, no community spirit. But Ethel's met him once or twice while taking the dog out for a walk, haven't you dear?"

Yes she had and he seemed friendly enough, although she had never really taken to the Irish.

Then there had been more questions. Had they seen many visitors? Did the man called Kelly keep strange hours? Had they seen anything at all unusual within the last few weeks?

Unfortunately, they had not been able to help, but Smith had smiled and put them at their ease.

"Not to worry, we'll find out for ourselves. Right, well, we'd better let you go. I'm sure you've things to do. It's very good of you to let us use your house like this. I promise we'll be quiet and we'll try not to get under your feet. Just one last thing. Could we have your back-door key? We'll be working round the clock, three shifts, nine of us altogether, and, since we can't keep popping in through the front in case we draw attention to ourselves, we'll need to make some copies."

Tom had handed it over and they had left him to get on with whatever it was that they did. Not quite able to restrain her curiosity, Ethel had kept popping up with trays of tea and sandwiches, questioning them on how things were progressing. The response was always polite but non-commital and eventually, with some difficulty, Tom had persuaded her to leave them in peace.

Although the Mawdsleys had no clear idea of who their guests were, they actually belonged to the Watcher Service, an integral part of 'A' Branch, MI5, who were based in Grosvenor Street, W1. Their duties covered a broad spectrum ranging from shadowing members of foreign embassies engaging in activities imcompatible with their diplomatic status, to keeping tabs on the political left. Not surprisingly, the Watchers were subjected to long hours of unalleviated boredom – what those in other departments mockingly described as an increased potential for leisure – but each peeping-tom was picked for his or her ability to cope and, in the organisation, their patience was legendary.

They had just logged Kelly's departure when the relief team ambled in. They were led by a man called Jackson, a burly man with a bristling 'tache and a passion for crossword puzzles.

"About bloody time!" said Smith, stretching the kinks from his back. "What kept you?"

"Well, we knew you were on the night-shift so your wife said I could stay."

Every day it was something new. If it wasn't "Does your wife know what you do nights? Does she believe you?", it was "Try Nivea for the wrinkles and some liposuction for those bags under your eyes." Quite the comedian was Jackson, but Smith was too tired to play the game.

"All right, boys, let's wrap it up and leave it to the amateurs."

But for Smith the day was not yet over. He dropped his team at Grosvenor Street, then pressed on through the early traffic to make his report to Harry Thomson. Not that he had anything to say except that he was tired, bored and thoroughly pissed off, and could he please have a transfer to MI-bloody-6 who at least had the benefit of spooking underneath a foreign sun.

"Morning, Bill."

The Director of 'K' Section was already busy with the mound of files upon his desk.

"Not for me it isn't, sir."

"Don't worry, we'll keep it brief. Just give me your progress up to date."

Smith slumped down in the chair which Thomson waved him to and rubbed his tired eyes.

"Just the same as yesterday. Absolutely nothing. No sign of Brady. Kelly arrived about half-seven and left twenty minutes later."

"Not very promising."

"No, sir. But it's still early days."

"What about the intercept?"

"They haven't touched the 'phone."

"Bugs?"

"Much the same. Brady's there by himself most of the time and watches too much telly. But Kelly seems to have spent the night with a woman. Said something about her begging him to let her help when he had given her a lot of bullshit about a brother he doesn't have on trial for terrorist offences."

"Do we know who she is?"

"Haven't got a clue."

"Or what she wants to help him with?"

Smith shook his head. "The only way we can cover all the bases is by getting Special Branch to lend us a few bodies."

"Yes, well, I'm afraid that won't be possible just yet. Nothing's gelled and until it has I'd rather keep the size of things down to a manageable level."

"Whatever you say, sir."

Perhaps it was a case of fatigue overriding caution, but Smith's response was noticeably sharp.

"You disagree with my decision?"

"It's not my place to say, sir."

"You're right, it isn't!" Thomson snapped. Then he continued in a more reasonable tone. "Look, Bill, in a perfect world we'd have this wired up so tight they wouldn't be able to fart without us hearing it. But at this stage we don't know what they're going to do and if we increase the scale of this operation there's a bloody good chance we'll signal our presence and blow the whole show.

"As things stand we know where they've stashed the arms and some of the people involved. Both locations are under round-the-clock surveillance and if there's any sign of movement we'll know. But to build a frame now for a picture whose contents and dimensions are unknown could prove a foolish and costly mistake. All we can do at this point is to make sure that we're prepared and when we know what they're about we have the resources to deal with them."

Smith nodded, but he wasn't entirely convinced. An increase in manpower would mean they were able to keep a firm grip on the job and it was better to be safe than sorry. Still, Thomson had a point; too many cooks had spoiled the broth of other operations in the past: but there was no place in a high-stakes game for timidity.

He climbed to his feet. "Will that be all, sir?"

Thomson nodded. "Yes, for now. Go home, get some sleep and I'll see you in the morning."

When he had gone, Thomson sat back with a sigh. He wasn't in the habit of explaining himself to subordinates and the experience had bitten through his humour. He knew how his decision to maintain the present staffing-level must have seemed to the men in the field; but something – call it instinct – had persuaded him to caution, and to those who lived in the shadows it was sometimes all there was.

"Sir ...?"

"What is is, Jamie?"

"The file you asked me to put together on all the known tip-offs from Perseus." He handed it to Thomson. "The early stuff's not up to much, but the last three years are dynamite if you'll pardon the pun."

"I'll read it later. Now bring me up to speed on the other jobs I gave you."

"Well, Frank Davis faxed the last message from Perseus and I've just taken it in to Bob Eyre to see if he can make anything of it. I also told Frank that you wanted to see him and he's flying up tomorrow morning. Wasn't too chuffed, though – said it was bloody inconvenient."

"Tough."

"One last thing, sir. Night controller got a call from Colonel Harris in Lisburn. He wanted to know how we're progressing with Perseus. What shall we tell him?"

A host of choice rejoinders sprang to Thomson's tongue but he swallowed them.

"Tell him we're ... progressing," he said, "and that when we've something to report we'll notify him immediately."

Daniels closed the door behind him and Thomson muttered an oath. He had only known about this Perseus character for a couple of days and already the army was making a bloody nuisance of itself. It really was too much! Did this Colonel Harris think he had nothing else to do? Each file in the mound before him represented an ongoing operation; and there was the added burden of having to investigate rumours that a Cabinet Minister was tupping a tart with dicey connections. The PM, no less, had ordered them to have a look into that one and by the pedigree of the plot priority had been established.

A knock at the door which opened to reveal a portly man with a balding head and thick-lensed glasses perched on an inadequate nose.

"Busy, Harry?" Bob Eyre asked.

"Just hiding," Thomson replied with a grimace at his workload. "What can I do for you?"

Eyre waved a sheet of flimsy paper. "This code young Daniels gave me."

"You can't have cracked it already?"

Eyre chuckled. "I might be a genius, but I'm not omniscient! No, what I came in to tell you was that we're out of luck on this one."

"What do you mean 'out of luck'?"

"We've identified the nature of the code, but unless we have the key the trunk stays closed." He shrugged. "Look, Harry, this is a number code, right? Well, each series of numbers represents a word. Nothing very unusual about that, of course; but since you've only given us a single specimen to work with, we can't expect to find the links in the numerical chain. It's just too difficult."

"You must be able to do something?"

"At best we could fish for identical sequences, assess the frequency of some of the figures and try to relate them to the most commonly occurring letters in the English language. But what's to say it even breaks down into English? What if it's in Russian or Arabic?"

"It's English."

"Are you sure?"

Thomson nodded. "Quite sure."

"Well, that's one less intangible to deal with. But then there's the possibility of it coming from a one-time pad, and if that's the case, we've definitely had it, because the key's continually changing."

"It's not from a one-time pad, either."

Eyre was flabbergasted. "You seem to know an awful lot about what it isn't, Harry! Suppose we start again, but this time tell me everything you think I need to know."

Briefly, Thomson sketched in the facts and watched as they sunk in.

"Well, that certainly puts a different complexion on it, doesn't it?"

"Does it?"

"Of course it does! We've been looking on it as though it were some highly sophisticated system, not some playground code intended for someone with no cryptographical training!"

"Does that mean you can break it?"

"It certainly narrows down the types of code we should be looking at. But if it's what I think it is, then no – I'm afraid I can't. Do you like literature, Harry?"

"What's that got to do with anything?"

"In this case probably everything. But you still haven't answered the question."

"Yes, I like to read although I don't get that much time for it."

"And how many books do you think there are?"

"Look, I don't see what—"

"Millions, right?" said Eyre, cutting in. "And I think this is a book-code. Look at the groupings," he said, laying the sheet on the desk and jabbing at it. "See the way they're presented? If I'm right and this is a book-code, they indicate page numbers, line numbers and word numbers. But unless we know what book he's using — and the edition because the format's always changing — we haven't a hope in hell of rendering it back into words. Do you see?"

Thomson saw.

"But you've already got a clue: the agent's codename — Perseus — and the fact that the operation was called Gorgon. Greek myths, Harry boy — Tyndall was crazy about them! If you want to read this cipher, I suggest you ransack his library."

With a final word about it being impossible to do his job without being given all the relevant data, the little cryptoanalyst departed.

Thomson felt like he had been bull-dozed. First Smith had criticised his judgement; now Bob Eyre had scolded him as if he were an errant schoolboy. All-in-all, a lousy start to the day!

Find the book and you find the key. That would mean his having to pay a visit to Tyndall's widow. He had been to their place in the country a few times, most recently for the funeral.

A classical scholar, Tyndall had been bibliomaniacal and the prospect of hunting through his shelves was alarming. However, he could always delegate, let some other poor bugger sweat it out — Lord knew he had enough on his plate as it was without adding to the burden! But then he decided he had better do it himself; apart from the fact that Monica knew him, his self- esteem was feeling bruised and he wanted to bring it back up to par.

No time like the present.

Reaching across the desk, he pushed a button on the intercom.

"Fiona, get Monica Tyndall on the line."

CHAPTER 9

CHARDONAY was a sprawling throwback to the last days of the Empire. A three-storey mansion set in five-hundred acres of prime woodland, it was reached by negotiating a winding tree-lined driveway to a gravelled forecourt with a sculptured stone fountain set in a circular pond in the centre. Monica Tyndall lived here with her daughter, Penelope, who had moved back in when William had died. It was far too big for the two of them, but Monica had grown up here and Penny had supported her reluctance to sell.

Harry Thomson parked before the entrance and sat a moment listening to the silence. It was such a peaceful place, not in the least imposing despite its great size. What signs of disrepair there were lent it an air of threadbare gentility; it was homely, yet grand — like a duchess with the common touch — and seemed to welcome all who chanced upon it.

Chardonay had only been out of the family's keeping once. In 1942, SOE had taken it over as a training base for agents destined for France. If one looked closely, the marks of occupation were still visible; at the rear of the house was a twenty-foot bank which had served as the shooting range, and on either side were hollows which showed where the air-raid shelters had been.

Monica had followed her father into the Service (or the 'College' as MI5 had then been known) where she had met and married William, a young Oxford graduate in 'D' Branch (Counter-Espionage) with a promising future. Then had come the family — two daughters and a son — and she had left her job to raise them. Kitty, the eldest, was now living in Australia with her husband and Bill junior was reading law at Cambridge; Penelope, the baby, had dropped-out of college and moved to London, but returned to keep her mother company when her father had died.

These had been the countdown years for Monica and William. With the family fledged and flown, it was a time for them to put into motion all the wonderful things they had planned. But one morning she had wakened to find him sleeping in his study — at least she thought he had been sleeping, but in fact he had been dead.

It was a peaceful demise, the doctor had assured her, a quiet passing in his sleep without him knowing a thing. Of course, she had been grateful that he had not suffered; he had always been afraid of death — or more particularly the manner of death. At least he hadn't died slowly like some they had known, lingering in constant pain, growing weaker every hour, until the scythe had finally severed the thread, releasing them into the arms of a welcome peace.

It was only after the burial that she had suddenly become aware of a savage vacuum which threatened to suck the life from her. But Penny had helped. Whenever she felt lonely and disconsolate, the daughter with whom she had so often fought would be there by her side to pull her out of it. Even death had benefits, for it had done what life could not: it had drawn them together, forging a bond upon the knowledge of what they had lost.

Deciding it was time to stir and, although he was reluctant to lose the moment, Thomson clambered from his car and thumbed the bellpush. He didn't have to wait very long. Monica answered the door herself. Tall and still as striking as ever, she took his breath away.

"I thought you'd forgotten all about me, Harry," she said, presenting her cheek to be kissed. "You'll stay for lunch?"

"What are you having?"

"Lord knows! Penny's turn today. So don't expect anything too prosaic."

She took his arm and led him into the drawing room, french windows open to the terrace and lawn. It was modestly furnished in a mixture of styles, but mostly modern as so many quality pieces had been sold for the upkeep of the place.

"Tea?" she asked.

Thomson nodded and she glided into the kitchen. He chose a seat beside the window. A warm breeze carried the scent of rural Surrey to his nose and his ears were lulled by the ticking of a long-case clock in the corner by the door.

Strange how everything connected with his job seemed so remote. It was almost as if the very walls of Chardonay were able to protect those who had ventured within from the things which troubled them the most. Thomson had often heard of places having their own character, but he had always thought the idea rather fanciful. His life seemed to bounce between his tiny flat in Kensington and the sterile environment of his office. But sitting here in the sunlight and the silence, he was overwhelmed by a sense of peace and was struck most forcibly by the difference. It made him feel uneasy. Rising, he stood and wandered slowly out on to the terrace, and a few minutes later Monica returned with the tea.

"Good idea!" she said. "We'll have it out here."

She placed the tray on the wrought-iron table and poured.

"How many sugars do you take now, Harry?"

"None," he replied, patting his belly. "I'm on a diet."

"Aren't we all, dear? God, but it's a lovely day."

Earl Grey, a lovely day, upon the breeze the scent of hay. Thomson smiled. Was he developing a poetic streak? They sat and stirred their teas in silence, then Monica gave him a quizzical smile.

"Right, Harry, you said something about books?"

He gave her a brief account of what he was after and why.

"Oh dear, that was rather silly of him, wasn't it?" she said when he had finished. "Unprofessional, not like him at all. I can't imagine what he was thinking of. So, you want to take a stroll around the library to see if you can find it?"

"Yes."

"I'd better give you a hand, they're in an awful jumble. For an orderly man, he built a most disorderly collection."

"And a large one, I believe?"

"Monstrous. Wall-to-wall. I suppose there must be fifteen thousand all-told."

Thomson grimaced. "Fifteen thousand ...?"

"Oh, come on!" she chided. "Surely you're not afraid of a few silly books?"

They finished their tea then Monica rose, filling her lungs and expelling the air with a huff of determination.

"Right," she said. "Let's get cracking."

Reluctantly, he followed her back indoors.

In spite of the number of volumes it contained, the library wasn't really very big. Heavy brown drapes were drawn across the mullioned windows, a leather-topped desk and executive swivel-chair dominated the area before them, and ranged against each wall, to a height of maybe fifteen feet, were rows and rows and rows of books, colourful, weighty and daunting.

"Right, I'll start at the far end," Monica said. "You might as well start here by the door. There's only one set of steps, I'm afraid, so we'll have to share them, unless you feel like rummaging in the cellar for a ladder?"

"Sharing's fine."

"I thought you'd say that." She laughed. "Oh, Harry, do try and smile!"

"How's this?"

"Desperate."

It was an honest reflection of what he was feeling and he turned away with a sigh.

Books, books, nothing but books, old books, new books, big books, small books. His eyes seemed to ricochet off the spines until his head began to spin. Dickens, Hardy, Trollope, Scott, Tolstoy, Flaubert, Zola ...

Why in the hell hadn't Tyndall put them into some kind of logical sequence? Biting back a curse he made a slow count to ten and continued.

"How's it going?" Monica asked when she had reached the end of her section. "No joy here, I'm afraid; just a couple of books on Viking and Chinese mythology. But I have found a rather splendid treatise on gardening."

"Did he actually read all these?"

"Oh, yes."

"However did he find the time?"

"I know; it's remarkable, isn't it? I think it had something to do with the fact that he grew up an only child. His father was a very distant man, reserved to the point of coldness. I remember the first time I met him he frightened me, so you can imagine what it did to Bill as a child.

"I suppose you could say books to him were a kind of escape. I used to tease him saying he preferred them to people and he never contradicted me. Funny really how we got together – him so solitary and me the exact opposite."

"Perhaps that was the attraction?"

"You could be right. But this isn't helping us find that wretched book."

As she moved to the next section, Thomson saw her raise a hand to her eye. The pain of her loss was obviously still very sharp and he considered suggesting to her that she leave the rest of the search to him. But she would only have refused, told him not to be so silly, so he carried on as if he hadn't noticed, and a few minutes later his eyes were drawn to a hardback shelved a foot above his head.

"Bingo!"

"What have you got?"

"A copy of Greek Myths by Robert Graves."

"Well, that's one, anyway – but what about the rest?"

What indeed? he thought, laying it on the floor and turning back to press on with the hunt. Then one became two and by the end of the search they had discovered seventeen.

"Right, what now?" Monica asked, stretching and rubbing her back.

Thomson sat behind the desk and withdrew the fax of Perseus's last message.

"We try and make some sense of this. If I call out the numbers can you look them up?"

"Sure."

She took the first book from the pile and when Thomson saw she was ready he began.

"Page 17 ... line 14 ... word 5."

"'Of'," she said, tracing her finger across the page.

"Page 76 ... line 3 ... word 2."

Repeating the process, she shook her head. "Sorry, Harry, but it looks like we'll have to try another book."

So they did and it still didn't make any sense.

Half-an-hour later, she closed the last one with a thud. Thomson rose and returned the fax to his pocket, his disappointment evident.

"Are you sure these are the only books he had on Greek mythology?"

"Bibliophiles aren't like alcoholics, Harry — they don't hide books in the cistern. If he had any more they'd be here with all the others."

He nodded, then Monica took him by the arm.

"Come on," she said, "it's nearly time for lunch."

It was almost two o'clock when he walked back out to his car. Monica had been right about the meal: it was anything but prosaic. A Kaleidoscope Salad for starters, followed by a main course of Worcestershire Beef, and for the sweet a Citroen Champagne Sorbet, all washed down with a bottle of chilled Chablis.

Every disappointment had its upside ...

"I'm sorry it didn't work out," Monica said. "But something will turn up, you'll see."

"I hope you're right."

"Of course I am. Now kiss me goodbye."

He did then clambered behind the wheel and twenty minutes later as he was tooling up the M3 wondered whether Bob Eyre had been wrong, that it wasn't a book-code. But right or wrong he had more pressing things to worry about, like the genesis of a new campaign of terror by the Provisional IRA. What the hell were they up to now? Soft-targeting? Strategic hits? Or another round of indiscriminate bombings? Maybe Smith was right; perhaps he should beef-up the surveillance? God, what a bloody gamble the whole thing was!

Patrick Kelly got back to the house in Gordon Road at seven o'clock. He looked exhausted, having priced a job in Harrow in the morning and finished building the wall for the tart whose payment had included yet another gruelling hour in the sack.

"Donal ...?"

There was no response. He ducked his head round the living room door, but Brady was nowhere to be seen. He called again, this time up the stairs, but still there was no reply. Going into the kitchen for a beer he saw why: the back door was open and Donal was sitting in a folding chair in the garden.

"Donal, will ye have a beer?"

Brady raised the bottle in his hand in reply so Kelly just got one for himself, knocking the cap off on the corner of the worktop, and wandered out to join him.

"Well?" Donal asked. "D'ye get it?"

Kelly reached into the breast pocket of his shirt and triumphantly withdrew a folded sheet of paper.

"What did I tell ye?" he said. "Hook, line an' sinker. I think I'll give it all up an' go on the stage!"

Ignoring him, Donal put down his beer and quickly scanned the list.

Nigel Barrett, Major, Signals, presently stationed in Germany ... Alan Pennick, Major, G1 Intelligence retired, freelance lecturer and author of military history and living in Surrey ... Inspector John Leahy, RUC Special Branch, deceased ... Peter Wilcox, Captain, 22 SAS, retired, running a private security firm and living in Ealing ... and finally, William Tyndall, former director of 'K' Branch, MI5 –

Suddenly, Donal pitched forward as he read the word 'deceased'. Was that the reason for the note left at the drop in which he was urged to make contact?

"Jayzus, Donal, are ye all right?"

"Aye, I'm fine ... t'was a bloody wasp that's all."

Kelly hadn't heard it and looked nervously about him.

Looking down the list once more, Donal made a lightning assessment of his predicament. Of the five men who could have identified him, two were dead, one was safely out of reach in Germany, which left two who could deliver him to Kennedy. Reilly's snatch-squad would be ready in a couple of days, which gave him four, five days at the most in which to disappear.

His heart was thumping and he found it hard to swallow. All the pieces were tumbling into place and the countdown for survival had begun.

Tyndall dead – his life-line frayed – the en claire message at the drop. Something was wrong, he had to reach his contact; ashen, he returned indoors to pack.

CHAPTER 10

THE room above the pub had been cleared of all extraneous furniture. All that remained was a long refreshments table set a few feet back from the furthest wall and three wooden chairs ranged in a semi-circle before it.

Three men sat at the table and in front of them another two were sitting in the chairs, the empty one between them. Their purpose: a court-martial. An informer had been hunted down and these proceedings had been convened to try him.

Presiding over the trial was Jim O'Hara, officer commanding the Belfast Brigade. On either side of him sat Danny O'Leary and Kiefer O'Toole, his lieutenants. Facing them were Michael Flaherty, Counsel for the Prosecution, and Liam Maguire, Counsel for the Defence. And by the door stood Timmy Finnegan, a burly man with a nose like flattened putty, a former boxer assigned to the court as Bailiff.

Assuring himself that all was prepared, O'Hara said: "Bring in the accused."

Finnegan opened the door and a moment later, flanked by two guards, the defendant entered the room and was marched to the chair in the centre. Counsel rose and O'Hara rapped the table with a gavel.

"This court is now in session. Be seated."

At a nod from O'Hara, Danny O'Leary opened the notepad before him.

"It is charged," he read, "that on the fourteenth o'this month, the accused, David Daniel Mullen, was observed in the company of an enemy Intelligence officer an' was witnessed givin' t'the said Intelligence officer a piece o'paper which was later established t'contain information of a nature that could prove injurious t'the Republican Movement.

"On bein' taken into custody, the accused admitted t'havin' met with the said Intelligence officer on a number o'previous occasions for the purpose o'supplyin' information for money.

"It is the contention o'the Prosecution that the accused acted knowingly in a manner which was harmful t'the lawful activities o'the Republican Movement, an' that, furthermore, he acted in direct contravention o'the oath he had taken when swearin' his allegiance to its service."

"David Daniel Mullen," said O'Hara. "How d'ye plead?"

"For God's sake, I never meant—"

"Guilty, or not guilty?"

"Christ Jesus!"

"Answer the question."

Mullen looked desperate. "I had no choice!"

"Let it be noted that the accused entered a plea o'guilty," said O'Hara. "Proceed."

Flaherty rose. "If it please the court, I'd like t'call as my first witness Mister Joseph Kearney."

"Bailiff."

Finnegan opened the door and a moment later an elderly man shuffled in.

"The witness will state his full name for the record."

"Joseph Patrick Kearney."

"Continue, Mister Flaherty."

"Mister Kearney, would ye please tell the court what ye saw take place on the night o'the fourteenth?"

"I was in havin' a wee dram in the pub. T'was a lovely night an' me wife—"

O'Hara raised a hand to interrupt him. "Jus' stick t'what's relevant if ye please, Mister Kearney."

"Yes, sir. Well, like I was sayin', I was in havin' a dram when I saw him—"

"The accused?" asked Flaherty.

"Aye — comin' in with a man I later heard t'be a Brit."

"An' what happened then?"

"They bought drinks at the bar, then slipped off to a table in the corner. Then he gave'm somethin'."

"The accused gave somethin' t'the man he was with?"

Kearney nodded.

"An' what was it ye saw him give?"

"T'was a piece o'paper."

"An' then what happened?"

"Well, when the Brit'd glanced at the paper, he took some money from his pocket an' handed it t'him — t'the accused."

"Ye saw him give some money t'the accused?"

"I did."

"An' what happened then?"

"They finished their drinks an' left."

"Thank ye, Mister Kearney," Flaherty said, then turned to the Defence. "Your witness."

Liam Maguire rose. "Mister Kearney, how old are ye?"

"Seventy-one."

"Is your eyesight good?"
"I've glasses that I'm like t'wear."
"An' were ye wearin' 'em on the night in question?"
"No, I don't think I was."
"So, what ye're sayin' is that ye wear glasses but on that night ye hadn't got 'em on. An' yet ye say ye saw the accused exchangin' somethin' for money. Are ye sure of what ye saw?"
Kearney looked piqued. "I may need glasses, young fella, but I'm not blind."
"But ye could've been mistaken?"
"No."
"It was definitely money?"
"Yes. I saw'm take it an' stuff it in his wallet, guilty-like."
"No further questions."
"Thank ye, Mister Kearney," O'Hara said. "Ye can go now."
The old man shuffled out, then Flaherty rose.
Prosecution calls Fergus Kavanagh."
Presently, a furtive-looking youth crept in, stated his full name for the record, then Flaherty opened his examination.
"Mister Kavanagh, what position do ye hold in the Movement?"
"I'm an officer in the Intelligence Branch."
"Would ye tell the court how ye became interested in the accused?"
"Rumours reached the department that Mullen had been seein' a Brit agent."
"So, what did ye do?"
"We instituted a thorough investigation, put a watch on his movements."
"An' your results?"
"We collected photographic evidence t'support the rumours an', when we confronted him with it, he broke down an' confessed."
"He confessed." A statement. "An' would these be the pictures?" he asked, removing some enlarged black-and-white photographs from a buff-coloured envelope and showing them to Kavanagh.
"They are."
"Thank ye. Mister President, the Prosecution would like to enter these into the record." He handed them to O'Hara.
"That concludes the case for the Prosecution."
"Thank ye, Mister Flaherty. Mister Maguire?"
"No questions for the witness."
"Mister Kavanagh, ye may go."
A moment later, Maguire rose. "If it please the court the Defence would like t'call the accused, David Daniel Mullen."
"Accused will stand," O'Hara murmured.

Mullen obeyed, although his knees were trembling so violently it seemed likely that he would fall.

"Mister Mullen," Maguire said quietly, "how long were ye in the Movement?"

"Four an' a half years."

"Ye're a family man, I believe?"

Mullen cuffed away a sniff and nodded. "Aye — two wee uns."

"Tell me, Mister Mullen: are ye workin'?"

"No."

"An' why is that?"

"I lost me job."

"How long ago?"

"Five months."

"For what reason?"

"I'm a Catholic."

"Would ye tell the court how ye first made the acquaintance o'Lieutenant Stevens o'British Military Intelligence?"

"Some o'the boys'd blown a car. I was picked up in the street on me way home."

"They questioned ye?"

"Aye. An' battered me."

"Did any attempts at coercion take place while ye were in custody?"

"Yes."

"Would ye describe what happened?"

"I was told they were gonna stick it on me, say I done the car. They said I'd go down for a five-stretch, more if they could swing it — said they'd find some other things for me t'carry."

"So, ye folded — made a deal?"

Mullen nodded. "I had no choice."

"Ye were thinkin' o'your family, perhaps? How they'd manage without ye?"

Another nod. "Times've been hard, money tight — they'd never've got along."

"How long ago did ye first meet the lieutenant?"

"Three — maybe four months."

"An' all that time ye were supplyin' him with the information?"

Pause, then came the quiet response: "Yes."

"How much did he pay ye?"

"A tenner — sometimes more."

"Dependin', I guess, on the quality o'the information?"

"Yes."

"An' would ye say that the quality was generally good?"

"I tried not t'give ... I was threatened — he said I knew what'd happen t'me if I didn't play along."

"A final question, Mister Mullen. How d'ye feel about what ye've done?"

Overcome with fear and remorse, Mullen began to weep and fell back into his chair. Maguire turned towards the bench.

"No further questions," he said.

O'Hara was unable to hide his distaste of the accused man; nor were any of the others.

"Mister Flaherty?"

"No questions, Mister President."

"Right, Counsel will present their closing arguments."

Liam Maguire rose and in the silence they could hear Mullen's sobs. At a sign from O'Hara, the guards approached and positioned themselves behind him.

"Mister President, members o'the court," Maguire said, "no words o'mine — or indeed of any man — could possibly excuse what the accused has done. It's a heinous thing t'betray your friends, your country an' beliefs, an' t'peddle your honour for the sake of a few extra quid. But think on this: Mullen had lost his job — he was a family man, a breadwinner — an' a cruel but all too common stroke had deprived him o'the means o'supportin' 'em.

"Then came an accident o'chance. Walkin' home one night, a car-bomb exploded. The occupyin' forces picked him up an' subjected him t'cruel mistreatment an' threats. They told him he was goin' down for somethin' they knew he hadn't done. Like many before him, an' in spite o'his trainin', he broke down an' let them turn him round.

He should've gone t'see his Brigade Commander, told him what'd happened. But he didn't. The fear was too strong. An' as a result o'that fear he became an informer an' damned himself in the eyes and hearts of his countrymen. But can ye not see the remorse he's feelin' now?

"David Daniel Mullen is known t'all of us. We've served with him. We know him t'be a good man. He's done wrong an' he knows it. Punish him, yes — God alone knows he deserves it — but spare his life, let him live t'reflect on what he's done an' repent."

Maguire sat down and Mullen gave him a helpless look of gratitude. O'Hara let a moment pass, then nodded to Flaherty who rose.

"Ye're damn right he needs punishin' an' God isn't the only one who knows it! This man is a traitor, a tout who sold his comrades for gain. Known to us all? In light o'what we heard today, it seems we never knew him at all! David Daniel Mullen betrayed us an' there's an end to it.

"A family man, we're told — a good man. Well, what about the men he sold t'the Brits? They were family men, too! An' good men! An' now they're rottin' in gaol! An' all because this bastard was greedy an' weak!

"Spare him?" Let him live t'reflect an' repent?" He'd laugh an' think he'd got away with puttin' one over on us, an' he'd be right! This man is a traitor. If we spare his life it'll only encourage others t'follow his example, an' then where the hell'd we be?

"The Prosecution contends that the case against him is proved an' moves t'demand that the maximum penalty be applied. David Daniel Mullen is scum – he's like a cancer an' needs cuttin' out. We therefore demand that he be sentenced t'death."

Flaherty sat down and again there was silence. O'Hara looked at his lieutenants, O'Leary and O'Toole. Then each man picked up a pencil and began to write, a single word which would determine the fate of the man before them.

"The accused will rise," said O'Hara, collecting and reading the verdicts. "Have ye anythin' t'say before the court passes sentence?"

Trembling violently, all Mullen could do was whimper.

"David Daniel Mullen, it is the sentence o'this court that ye be taken from hence to a lawful place o'detention an' from thence to a place of execution—"

"No ...!"

"Ye have the right t'lodge an appeal an' if ye exercise that right, your case will be delivered to a higher authority whose decision will be final. D'ye understand?"

Mullen started forward, eyes wide with fear and disbelief, but the guards restrained him.

"Christ – this is madness! Ye can't kill me! Jesus! Please! Oh, God, have mercy! Please – have mercy!"

"D'ye wish t'lodge an appeal?" O'Hara asked.

Mullen nodded frantically. "Yes – oh God, yes!"

"Take him away," O'Hara said. "This court now stands adjourned."

Martin Kennedy read the report of the trial at the desk in his sitting room. A storm was brewing and the air was heavily burdened; and in the distance could be heard the ominous roll of thunder, a sound which made the windows rattle in their housings.

Reaching the end he found appended the appeal, a plea for clemency, for leniency, and his features hardened.

He picked up a red felt pen and lightning tore across the horizon as he wrote a single word upon it: DENIED.

It was dusk when they parked on the wasteground. Mullen was dragged, screaming, from the car, his cries muffled by the hessian sack tied loosely round his neck. While two men forced him to kneel in the mud, a third took up position behind him; producing a revolver, he thumbed back the hammer and fired.

The body was discovered the following morning. Cutting through the wasteground on his way to work, a man saw tyre tracks and what he thought was a bag of rubbish dumped thirty yards from the road. It was only when he got to within a few feet of it and saw it bore a placard with the word 'Tout' scrawled in thick black letters that he realised what it was and, fighting the urge to vomit, stumbled back the way he had come to telephone the police.

CHAPTER 11

PETER Wilcox had finally decided to get on with the paperwork. The boys were out on jobs and he would have the office to himself for most of the day. Bathed in sunlight pouring in through the steel-framed basement window, he felt more relaxed than he had for quite some time and reached for the first sheaf of papers.

The Cumberland Hotel in Hanwell. A grand name for a seedy place. Twelve rooms – three to a floor – and as Mike Travis would say, a doddle to enter. The owner, a little Kerryman named Flint, had asked them to strengthen the security. He had been broken into five times in the last twelve months and had finally decided it would be cheaper to secure the premises than it was to be continually replacing what had been nicked.

Jacko Tyler and Dizzy Greaves had priced the job at two grand. Flint had complained that it was far too steep and, pocketing their consultation fee, they had left him to decide what was more important: peace of mind or prayer. A few days later he had reluctantly accepted and the work was now under way.

Since Jacko's brother-in-law was in the trade, they were able to get materials at cost. The alarm system was the most expensive item and, scribbling down a few figures, Wilcox saw that they would make a profit of seven hundred pounds. Two hundred a piece for the boys and three hundred in the bank. Not bad for a couple of days work. And with two other jobs of a similar nature underway, it was the best week they had had for quite a while.

At half-past ten the entry-'phone buzzed and he picked up the receiver.

"Hello?"

"Mister Wilcox? Jamie Daniels. I rang yesterday. I'm afraid I'm a little early."

"Daniels ...? Ah, yes – the spook. Come in."

He pressed the entry button and a moment later a youthful-looking man stepped nervously through the door. Wilcox examined his Special Branch warrant card and, shaking hands, motioned the MI5 man to a chair beside the desk.

"Can I get you a coffee?"

"No thanks. I'm a bit pushed for time. If I could just ask you a few questions?"

"Fire away."

"Right. But first I have to remind you that you're still bound by the Official Secrets Act and that what we're going to discuss is covered by that Act. Okay?"

Wilcox looked amused. "Okay."

Daniels paused dramatically, then began.

"In 1984 you were involved in an operation called Gorgon."

Wilcox had been involved in many operations during his army career. Many of them had owned fanciful names and he cast a line back through his memory.

"Gorgon ... Gorgon ...?"

"A specialist team put together to run an informer in Ulster. The agent's codename was Perseus."

"I remember. What about it?"

"Well, William Tyndall died a few months ago without making contingency plans for handing over the running of his man. What we'd like to know is whether you've any information which could help us to re-establish contact."

"What do you mean 're-establish contact'? Surely the system's still in place? And why come to me? Why not ask his present handlers? They'll be able to tell you far more than I can."

"I'm afraid that won't be possible," Daniels replied. "When Tyndall returned to London, he dismantled the apparatus. There was only one man left with orders to forward any communications. Tyndall would decode them and pass the information back to G1 Intelligence."

"So what's the problem?" Wilcox asked. "Just have them redirected to Lisburn."

"I wish it were that simple."

"What do you mean?"

"We don't have the key to the cipher," Daniels replied.

Wilcox laughed. "Are you telling me that MI5 can't crack the bloody code?"

Daniels flushed. "I can see why you find it funny, but need I remind you that we have a man operating in hostile territory without support, without a safety-net? Now, when the operation was set up, you were the cut-out, the postman. You were the only man on the ground with whom he had any contact. Is there anything you can tell us about him? Did you meet him? Did you see him?

"If you're asking me if I know who he is, I don't," Wilcox replied. "Only Tyndall knew. We didn't have to. It was strictly need-to-know. But you have to appreciate how things were back then. The orthodox Intelligence system was falling to pieces – nobody shared, nobody co-operated – the result being that the Paddys were tripping over informers every day. Obviously something needed to be done. We couldn't afford to let things go the way they had been in the seventies.

"Then Tyndall had this bright idea: why not draw personnel from different Intelligence-related branches to run an agent with potential? Hence Gorgon. But when it was all set up and running, we were returned to our units. We assumed we were going to be replaced. But apparently not."

"No." Daniels rose. "Well, thanks for your time. Look, here's my card. If you do think of something, give me a call."

"Sorry I can't be more helpful," Wilcox said, showing him to the door.

When Daniesl had gone, he returned pensively to his desk. You could always trust Intelligence to screw things up; and this, it seemed, was yet another example of incompetence endangering the life of a source.

He knew how terrifying life could be for informers. And it wasn't a long life. They were always caught. But on the other hand, Perseus had been given a rare opportunity to wriggle off the hook, to walk away. Well, bloody good luck to him, Wilcox thought, reaching for another sheaf of papers.

Frank Davis caught the noon shuttle from Aldergrove to Heathrow. He hadn't slept and felt as rough as his reflection in the toilet mirror suggested. An old man at forty, his pallor spoke of spending too much time indoors burning candles which seemed to get shorter every year. His deepset eyes were like dull brown buttons, his teeth were stained a dirty yellow from smoking too many cigarettes and his once dark hair had receded into thin grey feathers which curled untidily above his ears.

Like many MI5 men stationed in Ulster, Davis had been scarred by the experience. For five years he had haunted the shadows of a war which had not been officially acknowledged; the covert nature of his work had robbed him of the ability to believe in anything but the frailty of the human condition. The concepts of morality, of goodness and compassion were things that he had learned to disbelieve, and cynicism was ingrained in him to a degree he had never thought possible, with every fresh experience seeming to add another layer.

It hadn't always been that way. As a young man he had joined the Service believing in the work. He had believed in democracry and the necessity of undertaking whatever measures were called for to support it, however underhand they might have been. But gradually the paradox of using undemocratic methods to protect democracy had filtered through to his consciousness, and by then, of course, it was too late: the damage had been done. Whatever remained of his good intentions had been buried beneath the corpse of his conscience. There were no absolutes; there was no black and white: just a grey man doing a grey job in a grey world.

Physically, Davis was a ringer for the job. He wasn't tall, he wasn't striking; and if you were to see him in a crowd, you'd find your eyes slip by him like he simply wasn't there. His habitual form of dress was an old grey suit and a mac with a torn left loop where the belt had once been and a pair of comfortable brown brogues, scuffed but respectable. His ties were usually thin and of a neutral colour and apart from a pinkie ring, the only jewellery he wore, was a copper bangle he had been given for his rheumatism. Not that it worked. He only kept it for the memories it kindled. Karen Balshaw, a girl he had once loved; another casualty of the job which destroyed so much, until there was only the job.

There was a knock on the door.

"Sir, We'll be landing soon."

"Right," he said, zipping up his washbag and rinsing the whiskers from the sink.

He returned to his seat and was about to light a cigarette when a 'ding' drew his eyes up to the no smoking and fasten seatbelt signs. Reluctantly obeying, he settled back and felt his stomach lurch as the plane began its descent. He hated flying, surrendering control of his life to a stranger; and, as they broke through the louring clouds, he glanced uneasily at the toytown landscape beneath.

But it was soon over and five minutes later he was walking through the Customs point where Jamie Daniels was waiting to take him to Curzon Street.

"Remember now," said Patrick Kelly. "Give my love t'Moira an' the kids."

"Take care o'yourself."

"Always."

"Cheers."

Donal carried his suitcase outside.

"That was a short stay, Mister Brady," said Seamie, slinging his case into the boot. "D'ye not like London."

"Does anyone?" Donal asked, getting into the car.

"Me, I love it." Seamie clambered in beside him and fired the engine. "But I have t'admit it'd be a much better place without the Brits!"

In the house across the street, Jackson spoke into his radio.

"All, yours, Tango Three. Don't lose them."

"Roger, Alpha."

A red Ford Escort parked at the end of the block drove off in pursuit.

Turning left into the one-way system round Haven Green, both vehicles vanished from sight.

"Entry in the log," said Jackson to the man who sat beside him. "Target left premises 10:14 a.m. Get it?"

"Got it."

"Good."

With regular reports on their journey to the airport crackling into the Gordon Street o.p., Tango Three notified Alpha when they were square-wheeled at the destination.

"Target leaving car, now. Driver remaining. Who do we tag? Please advise. Over."

"Stay with Target. Repeat. Stay with Target," Jackson replied.

"Roger Alpha. Car departing. Target entering terminal. Am in pursuit. Out."

"Bit bloody risky," said the man with the log. "We know where Brady's going, don't we?"

"When a player leaves the board you need to make sure he's out of the game," Jackson replied. "Last thing we need is him legging it down to the underground to a safehouse we know nothing about."

Donal bought a paper and a coffee while he waited for his flight to be announced. If there were no delays, he could expect to be in Belfast by half-twelve. In his pocket was a small address book filled with items from a telephone directory and the residential details of the only two reachable men who could finger him.

At eleven o'clock, the announcement was made. He picked up his case and crossed the terminal to UK Departures, Gate 1. Following discreetly, Tango Three made sure that he had boarded the aircraft before he used his radio.

"Alpha, this is Tango Three. Target has departed."

"Roger, Tango Three. Come home to mother. Out."

One more task remained and Jackson reached for his cellular 'phone.

"Hello?"

"Jamie? Tom Jackson. Brady's gone."

"I'll tell the boss."

Jackson rang off. The Irishman was someone else's problem now.

Seventy minutes after leaving Heathrow, BA Flight 9715 touched down at Aldergrove. Twenty minutes later Donal Brady took a black cab home and did not know that he was being followed.

CHAPTER 12

FRANK Davis left Thomson's office barely able to restrain the impulse to slam the door behind him. Their meeting had begun well enough; but gradually the veneer had cracked and he was damned if he were going to carry the can for Tyndall's unprofessionalism.

Thomson's secretary, Fiona, gave him a sympathetic smile as he strode past on his way to the corridor and lift. He had been told to visit 'A' Branch for the keys to a nearby Service flat where he was to remain until a meeting regarding Operation Gorgon with the DG could be arranged. And how bloody long will that take? he had asked, mindful of his duties back in Ulster. A day or two, Thomson had replied; and Davis had left with the nasty feeling that he was being hung out to dry.

Two hours later, after a long hot bath, he was sitting in a white terrycloth robe beside a window overlooking Hyde Park. The flat, which was easily worth a couple of hundred grand, was used by MI5 to house dignatories and defectors. Was this by way of being his 'last cigarette' before his career was shot to pieces? Or was it customary practice to fling open the doors of such luxury to field agents as low in the Organisational matrix as himself? Somehow, he didn't think so and, determined to make the most of it, he turned the key in the drinks cabinet and poured himself a rum.

At five o'clock, the doorbell rang. Roused from his slumber on the long leather couch, he rose and padded across the deep-piled carpet to the door where he squinted through the spy-hole. It was Thomson's man, Daniels. Reluctantly, he let him in and went back into the lounge, the younger man following with an appreciative whistle as he took in the surroundings.

"Talk about roughing it," he said. "Are you sure you can cope?"

"I've known worse."

"Think I'll put in for a transfer if this is what you get."

Davis was tired. "What can I do for you ...?"

"I've news about your interview with the DG."

"I'm listening."

"Friday morning, ten o'clock."

"Friday" But that's two days away!"

Daniels shrugged. "Earliest it could be managed, I'm afraid."

Davis was furious. Were his other commitments supposed to go hang?

"Where's Thomson now?" he demanded, reaching for the 'phone. "Is he still in his office?"

"I wouldn't do that if I were you – he's in a foul mood. And anyway, you won't be able to change anything."

"Maybe not, but it'd make me feel a hell of a lot better!"

"I don't see why you're getting so worked up. Seems to me you'd welcome a break from Belfast."

"And what the hell would you know about it?"

Daniels raised his hands, palms out. "Look, Frank, I'm only the messenger. If you want to have a go at someone, find somebody else, okay?"

Davis sighed. "Sorry."

"Forget it. Do you fancy a pint?"

"Keeping tabs on the condemned man?"

"The only tab I keep is in the pub around the corner."

"Give me a minute to get dressed," Davis said and vanished into the bedroom.

Donal Brady had only been home a couple of hours when one of Kennedy's stooges came to collect him. Apprised of all that had happened in London, the Chief decided it was time to get things moving.

"Reilly won't like it," Donal warned. "His trainin' time's been cut t'the bone as it is."

"Reilly doesn't have t'like it jus' so long as he does as he's told," Kennedy replied. "If he gives ye any shit ye can tell him t'keep it for me."

"I'm sure that won't be necessary."

"It better bloody hadn't! I'm sick t'death o'listenin' t'complaints about sendin' green Vols into the field. Times is hard – we haven't the time t'train 'em like we used to – an' if the standards're slippin' it's the touts ye can blame, not the Army Council.

"Anyway, that's not the issue. I want ye t'go t'the playground. Billy McKee'll drive ye there. He's money an' tickets for the boat. Ye'll be the cut-out between Reilly an' meself. Stay in daily contact with him an' keep me informed. I want t'know what progress he makes an' when he has the job done."

"Right."

"Away now, Donal, sooner started, sooner ended. An' mind ye hide them tickets well before ye cross the border."

Donal nodded and, letting himself out, returned to the car where Billy McKee was waiting.

A little after six o'clock they parked beside the barn and made their way along the muddy track to the farmhouse.

"Tim ...?" Donal called. "Tim, are ye there ...?"

There was no response and they went inside to wait for the cell to return.

It was almost half-past seven when they heard a banging at the front. Distracted by the noise they almost dropped with fright when behind them, from the entrance to the kitchen, came the metallic click of a pistol being cocked. It was Reilly.

"Jayzus, Tim, ye stupid bastard!" Donal cried. "What the fuckin' hell d'ye think ye're playin' at?"

"Did we scare ye, Donal?"

"What d'ye fuckin' think? Christ God Almighty!"

Reilly lowered his weapon and turned to the young man standing behind him.

"Peter, tell Jimmy he can let up on the door now, or our guests'll be gettin' a headache as well as brown trousers."

With a grin the young man departed and Reilly lay his gun on the sideboard. Even through the camouflage stripes on his face the marks of weariness were visible.

"Okay, Donal. When d'we go?"

No anger, merely resignation. Donal was surprised.

"Tomorrow mornin'."

"How?"

"Boat. I've the tickets here in my pocket."

Laughter from the hallway, then the three young men walked into the room. Not one of them looked over twenty.

"Ye've not met the lads," said Reilly. "Tall one's Jimmy Gilvarry—"

Tall, fair, with a boyish mien.

"The ugle one's Peter O'Connor—"

Striking blue eyes, with a vanity that was immediately apparent.

"An' the wee beggar's Ricky Farrell."

Didn't look a day over sixteen and seemed to melt behind the other two.

Nods were exchanged.

"Lads, Mister Brady's brought us some news. We go tomorrow."

Puppies couldn't have shown more excitement and Donal felt a sudden sense of regret.

Introductions made, Reilly waved them away. "Get cleaned up an' fix yourselves some grub." When they had gone, he reached for a bottle of Bushmills and two tumblers. "Right then, Donal, it's time ye prepped me up."

Half-an-hour later, Reilly pocketed the address book containing the locations of Kelly's safehouse and the two men they were to snatch.

"This Wilcox fella was SAS, ye say?"

Donal nodded.

"Ye're not afraid, are ye?" McKee asked, observing Reilly's reaction. "He's only one man."

"D'ye ever hear tell o'the Texas Rangers? Well, way back in the 1870s, the mayor o'West Texas had a riot on his hands. He telegraphed the Rangers' headquarters an' asked 'em to'send a company o'men. A coupla days later a single man stepped off the train with an overnight bag, a Winchester an' a Colt. "Where's the rest of 'em?" asked the mayor. 'There's just me,' said the man. 'But I asked for a company!' said the mayor. 'Why, so ye did,' said the Ranger, 'but there's only one riot ain't there?'"

"I think what Tim's tryin' t'say," said Donal, "is that ye should never underestimate the power o'one man."

"Especially when he's been in the SAS," Reilly added. "Afraid o'him? Ye're damn right I'm afraid. But if ye're so brave, why don't ye come along an' take'm yourself? I'm sure it could be arranged ..."

McKee, looking distinctly uncomfortable, rose. "I think it's time we was headin' back, Mister Brady."

Trying not to smile, Donal rose. "Aye, I think it probably is. Well, Tim, may ye die in Ireland."

"I won't get the chance t'die anyplace else unless ye give me them tickets."

"Christ Jesus, I'd forgotten all about 'em!"

He handed them over and Reilly led them out into the night.

"Don't forget, now, I'll ring ye every night at six o'clock," he said. "Startin' tomorrow t'let ye know we've arrived."

"So long, Tim."

They shook hands, then Donal and McKee returned along the muddy track to the car. Two-and-a-half hours and five checkpoints later they were back in Belfast driving along the Falls, McKee dropping Donal off and motoring away through the rain.

It was a curious thing being guided by Fate. For nine years Donal had lived with fear, expecting to feel the hand of the Organisation he had betrayed upon his collar; but now that the moment of discovery was drawing near he felt somehow divorced from what he was, what he had done and the danger he was facing. Of course, it was ironic that he had been charged to find himself; even more ironic that he was still a vital link in the chain. If the worst happened and he was taken before the Brits could pull him out, Kennedy would fall, bringing half the Army Council down behind him, for each Brigade would be howling for reconstruction. That was what it had all been about: to inflict maximum damage to the infrastructure and credibility of the Movement. Well, he had hurt it and no mistake. Tyndall would have been delirious; Tyndall, that cynical bastard who had set him on the path of betrayal.

Strange, but Donal no longer felt any animosity towards him. They were merely players in a game where there were not – nor could be any winners: everybody lost. It was really very simple: take a community and divide it – Catholics on one side and Protestants on the other – add hatred and politics, guns, bombs, soldiers and priests, stir thoroughly with a generous seasoning of conflicting needs and ideologies, bring to the boil and serve to a world so used to seeing and hearing about it that it no longer noticed or cared. The game even had a name – The Troubles – a low-key euphemism for War which suggested that the problem was merely a civil disturbance which occasionally got out of hand.

Occasionally ...?

He remembered Reilly's anecdote which illustrated how one man could make a difference.

One man. Even a tout ...?

Tout – what the hell was that? Just one more ingredient in the Six Counties recipe for pain. Even the word had lost its stigma, its power to shame. But Donal knew his present sense of apathy would fade; and when it did the fear would return and with it would come a renewed and stronger realisation of betrayal.

What then ...? Would fear and uncertainly lead him into betraying himself? Would the strain of living a lie become too much and would he seek release by surrendering to the inevitable? How would it end? Rescue, relocation and a chance to start again? Or a bullet through the back of the head on a lonely patch of wasteground?

Suddenly, he saw his apathy for what it was: a feeling of false calm, like the eye of a hurricane, that would leave him unprepared. It was something which had to be fought, to be overcome. To give up now would only invite an end which could – had to be – avoided. And what about Moira and the kids ...?

The IRA wasn't noted for taking reprisory action against the families of those who had betrayed it. But he had done an awful lot of damage. That being so his actions as an informer had probably jeopardised their safety. Realising this, he felt his apathy melt away to be replaced by a renewed sense of purpose. He had to contact the people who were running him, the ones who had taken over from Tyndall. However unwillingly, he had kept his end of the devil's bargain and the time for them to pay had finally arrived.

There was a 'phone box thirty yards away and, crossing the road, he jogged towards it pulling a handful of coins from his pocket. He dialled the number. Five rings ... ten ... a minute passed with no response and, hanging up, he wandered back out into the rain.

The time to pay ... The time to die ...?

Shivering, he pulled his collar up around his neck and slowly made his way home.

CHAPTER 13

TIM Reilly dropped his canvas travelling bag in the doorway and nodded.

"Not bad," he said.

A winding staircase climbed away to his left and before him stretched a long green passageway with white-painted panelled doors and framed Constable prints upon the walls.

"Hundred-an'-ten grand," said the rat-faced man with lank ginger hair. "I've another three in Hammersmith an' Fulham. Fire- damaged, but with great potential."

"Did your mommy never tell ye matches are dangerous?"

"We all have t'make a livin'."

"Ye're a greedy man, Patrick Kelly."

Jimmy Gilvarry, Peter O'Connor and Ricky Farrell stepped inside. None of them had managed to sleep and there was not a trace of their former ebullience.

"Will we take our things upstairs, Mister Reilly?" asked Gilvarry.

Reilly nodded. "Aye, an' try t'get some sleep while ye're up there."

Nervous as kittens first time in a garden they were and their tension was translating to him. Things were going to be tough enough without his having to coddle them on and the last thing he needed was their stress fastened on to his to impair his judgement.

"Sit yourself down in the front," said Kelly, "an' I'll make a pot o'tay."

The living room was spacious with blue papered walls and a high white ceiling. Reilly moved to the window and, drawing back the lace net curtain, cast a lingering glance at Gordon Road. It was peaceful. He let the curtain fall back into place and sat in the armchair in the corner; and five minutes later Kelly returned with a tray laden with a stainless steel teapot, a small jug of milk, a bowl of granulated sugar and two City of London tourist mugs.

He had already determined how much Kelly knew about the job they had to do on the drive from Euston: very little and anxious to keep it that way. That suited Reilly — the fewer people who knew, the better — and although it had been Kelly who had procured the addresses of the men they were to snatch he did not know what they intended to do with them when they had them.

When Kelly passed him his tea he told him they would be needing a car.

"No problem. I'll have Seamie drop one by tonight."

"An' a place t'question some bodies, somewhere quiet, remote, y'know, some place we're not likely t'be disturbed."

"Only place I have like that's a warehouse where I've stashed the arms."

"Take me there."

"What, now? But I've only jus' made the—" Reilly's expression told him protestation would be fruitless. He rose. "Okay, I'll jus' fetch me keys," he said, and a minute later they were walking towards his BMW.

Harry Thomson read the faxed report which had reached him that morning. Brady had been tailed to Martin Kennedy's farmhouse and across the border to a strip of land which was known to be a training camp for recruits to the Provisional IRA. Although the scenario was still unclear, the fact that it went right to the top was horribly apparent. It was unusual to be able to trace an operation to the Army Council — never mind directly to its Chief-of-Staff — and this suggested to Thomsom that whatever they were planning was important and that it was time to start worrying.

A knock on the door and Daniels entered.

"Message from Alpha, sir. Four men have just moved into the target house in Gordon Road."

"Do we know who they are?"

"Not yet, sir. Film's just been taken down to the lab for processing. As soon as we have some glossies we'll wire them to RUC Special Branch and see what they can tell us. But the latest news is that Kelly and the one who seems to be in charge have just left the house. Tango Three's dogging them."

"Thank you, Jamie. Keep me up to speed, will you?"

"Yes, sir."

Daniels left and Thomson fell back to musing.

An IRA arms shipment, an active service unit in place to do a job which had been sanctioned by the Provo Chief-of-Staff. The pieces were beginning to fall into place; but as Sherlock Holmes had said it was a capital mistake to theorize in advance of the facts, and until they had a fuller picture action was out of the question. So, what did they do? Nothing. Simply maintain the watching brief and gradually, as the saying went, their patience would be rewarded.

A verse from a poem he had once read sprang unbidden to his mind expressing a sentiment which might have persuaded a man of less experience into acting prematurely:

Act too early, show your hand;
Win the game but lose the strand.
Act too late and lose the lot;
A bloody nose was all you got.

But in this case, the price would be far more than a bloody nose!

Thomson had never been a gambling man, but if he had been he was certain that this was one time his money would have stayed in his pocket. With a sigh, he took a file from the stack before him and turned his thoughts to matters far removed from the activities of the Provisional IRA.

Kelly unlocked the warehouse door and led the way inside.

"Stuff's in the corner there, in the crates. D'ye want t'see it?"

Reilly shook his head. "Another time. Can ye get rid o'the van?"

"Get rid of it?"

"Shift it. It takes up too much room."

"Sure, I can park it round the back."

"Do it now."

Kelly didn't much like being ordered around, but didn't feel up to protesting. He opened the main doors and, jumping into the cab, drove the van outside.

"D'ye have any chairs?" Reilly asked when he returned.

"What kind o'chairs?"

"Straight-backed wooden ones like they used t'use in schools."

"I don't, but I daresay I can get some. How many d'ye need?"

"Two'll be fine."

"Right. Anythin' else?"

"A table an' a lamp, preferably anglepoise."

"When d'ye need 'em?"

"Tonight."

Kelly looked doubtful. "Tonight ..."

"Is that a problem?" Reilly asked in a tone which implied that it better hadn't be.

"No, no. Jus' — I mean, I'll do me best."

"Good. Can't ask for more than that, can I?"

A moment passed while Reilly took a final look around. Then he turned and headed for the door.

"C'mon, he said. "Let's go for a drive."

"Where to?"

"Frensham."

"Surrey?"

"Do I detect a note o'reluctant disbelief?" Reilly asked. "Cos if I do we'd better get a few things straight. One, you are now a part of an active service unit of the Provisional IRA. Two, I am the officer comman-din' this unit. An' three, we're here t'do a job an' if I say we go some-place, we bloody well go. Do I make myself clear?"

"Crystal."

"Good. Because I'd hate t'have t'revise my expectations of ye." Towering over the diminuitive Kelly, he placed his hand around the back of his neck. "I really would."

"I always did like the country," Kelly said, stepping back when he was released. "Cows, trees, all that fresh air — I can taste it already."

Locking up and returning to their car, neither man was aware that they were being observed and photographed from the office of a ware-house nearby. As they drove away one of the Watchers picked up his radio.

"Alpha, this is Bravo."

"Go ahead, Bravo."

"Target One and an unidentified male have just paid us a house- call."

"Did they raid the fridge?"

The arms shipment had been fitted with electronic devices designed to emit a signal when the crates were jemmied open.

"Negative, Alpha."

"Lab the film. And Bravo ...?"

"Alpha?"

"Have a nice day."

With a look of disgust Bravo tossed the laughing radio on the desk and, leaning back in the old wooden chair, wondered not for the first time why he always ended up at the uncomfortable end of things.

Alan Pennick was a balding man of average height but dangerously overweight. An hereditary heart condition had ended his army career when he had served as a major in G1 Intelligence and now he made his living as an author — and occasional lecturer — in military history.

Stress, the quacks had told him, was a thing to be avoided. Fortu-nately he had never married which took care of one major cause (or so he liked to say) but they had never mentioned dogs as being part of the pressure equation; and now, clambering breathlessly to the summit of the escarpment overlooking Frensham Little Pond, he cursed as he saw the collie already making its descent and followed, breaking into an in-voluntary run, pausing at the foot of the ridge for breath.

Like many unfit people Pennick wore the uniform of an athlete dur-ing his leisure hours, a shiny multi-coloured tracksuit and a pair of Ree-bok trainers. He knew it afforded others a sense of amusement, that he looked ridiculous; but he had stopped caring what others thought a very long time ago. He had been fit once. Very fit. As a young lieutenant he had undergone the gruelling selection course for the SAS. Of course, he had failed like so many of them did; but the very fact that he had tried had worked in his favour by bringing him to the attention of his superiors as being a man who had 'the right stuff'. The fact that he had also found time to take a degree in History and Economics had helped as well. But then his heart had played him false and his journey to the top had hit the downgrade.

He had left the army seven weeks before his fortieth birthday with an adequate pension and a marked inability to adjust to civilian life. Now he was forty-five and, though he had long since learned to cope, he missed being part of the Game, of the process of intelligence gathering and analysis.

But life had its compensations. Quite by accident he learned that he had the ability to breathe life back into the dead past. His first book upon the Crimean War had passed almost unnoticed; but his second upon the Battle of Waterloo had earned him great acclaim, especially since he had unearthed proof of a British plot to kidnap Napoleon on the eve of the battle led by a dashing young cavalry subaltern. Of course, the plot had failed and all who had taken part had died; but his discovery had opened up a whole new avenue of speculation which had rocked the groves of academe.

Some critics had dubbed him the Le Carre of the historical genre and the popularity of his work had secured for him an entirely new and welcome, if unexpected, career as a freelance lecturer. His affability and natural charm meant that he spent more time on the lecture circuit than was perhaps wise for one whose health was fragile; but Pennick had always been gregarious and, given the choice of communing with people or the typewriter, people won flat every time. Besides, the lecture circuit had become so lucrative that its loss would most certainly be felt.

By now the dog had reached the pond where she was slaking her thirst, the leaden water sparkling as it parried the sunlight.

"Come on, Jessie!" he called, taking the lead from his pocket; and a minute later they were heading back through the trees for home, the pine needles soft and springy underfoot and the air smelling fresh and green.

The cottage was secluded. Painted white, with a grey slate roof, it stood alone amid a stand of birch and pine. There was but a single approach road, if road it could be called, a tree-lined path which ran for half-a-mile, beginning at the car park for visitors to the ponds.

It was the perfect ground for a snatch.

Reilly and Kelly were on their way back to the car when they heard the barking of a dog. Taking cover, they saw an overweight man in a tracksuit making for the cottage through the trees on the other side of the path. He let slip the dog which gambolled about his legs before racing away to the cottage and they watched him go inside.

It never ceased to amaze Reilly how easy a target ex-servicemen could be. Perhaps they thought that once they had withdrawn from the Game they no longer had to worry. In most cases that was true; but there were exceptions – former SAS men and Intelligence officers in particular for they had made Ireland bleed – and Alan Pennick belonged body and soul to that category.

Reilly checked his watch. It was half-past four, an hour-and-a-half before he had to telephone Donal to notify him of their arrival and the beginning of the operation. They walked a little in the cover of the trees, Kelly losing his footing and cursing quietly, and were soon back in the car where they joined the traffic snaking slowly homeward.

CHAPTER 14

THEY came for him at midnight. Alan Pennick was wakened by a rapping on the front door and the sound of Jessie growling and snapping and scratching at the woodwork.

"All right, Jess, that'll do!" he said, coming into the hallway from the bedroom and fastening the cord of his dressing gown. Then, taking her by the collar, he called: "Who's there?"

"Police."

Police ...?

"What's it about?"

"Just open the door please, Mister Pennick."

"Do you know what time it is?" he demanded.

There was no reply. Changing hands on Jessie's collar, he cursed and flipped the catch on the lock. Suddenly, the door flew open, knocking him to the floor. In the dim porch light he saw four masked figures.

Jessie sprang at one of them, seizing him by the arm and dragging him down. The man screamed and one of the others aimed a vicious kick at the collie which thudded audibly into her ribs. She whined but did not release her grip. Pennick tried to rise to protect her, but was himself kicked back to the floor. Then he felt something being pressed to his face, some sort of pad impregnated with a pungent odour which began to rob him of his senses, the will to resist, the strength to fight.

His final sight, his last coherent thoughts before blacking out were of Jessie whose life was twitching away beneath the violent clubbing of feet.

Crying with pain, Peter O'Connor tore off his hood and raised his bloody fingers to his face. The dog had torn the flesh from his cheekbone and his right eye was blinded with blood.

Reilly bent down beside him and examined the wound. The youth would never pull the birds like he used to.

"Ricky, take him t'the bathroom, clean him up. Jimmy, help me get this bastard into a chair."

As Farrell helped O'Connor to his feet, Gilvarry and Reilly carried the unconscious Pennick into the front room where they dumped him into a chair.

"Fasten him down," Reilly ordered, producing a length of waxed cord; then he followed the sound of O'Connor's screams.

"How's he doin'?"

Farrell was trembling. "I — I dunno. He's bleedin' awful bad."

"Gimme that cloth — ye'll never stop it like that. Why don't ye go give Jimmy a hand."

Farrell obeyed and Reilly raked through the medicine cabinet above the sink until he found some iodine and a box of sticking plasters.

"All right, son, this is gonna sting. Be still, now."

O'Connor whimpered as Reilly cleaned out the wound, fixing two plasters at right-angles to pull the flesh together and a larger one lengthways over them to hold them in place. It was a hell of a mess and was going to need stitching. Then he turned his attention to the boy's arm. Fortunately, his padded jacket had minimised the damage. Washing away the blood, Reilly examined the puncture marks made by the dog's teeth. They were none of them too deep and the blood ran mainly from the inside of the forearm where the worrying-action had torn along a vein. He cleansed the wounds and covered them with plasters, then rose stuffing the used medical material into his pocket.

"Can ye stand?" he asked.

The youth nodded and Reilly aided him into the sitting room where Pennick was firmly secured to a dining-table chair.

"How's your man?" he asked.

Gilvarry shook his head. "I don't like the look of him. It's his breathin' — it's kind o'wheezy — an' his colour."

Reilly approached and gently raised the unconscious man's head. Gilvarry was right: he didn't look well at all.

"Ricky, go t'the bathroom — see if ye can find some smellin' salts."

Farrell obeyed and Gilvarry nodded across to where O'Connor was resting on the sofa.

"How's Peter?" he asked.

"He'll live," Reilly replied. "But I don't think he'll be goin' in for any beauty contests."

"Poor bastard."

Farrell returned with a small blue bottle of carbonate of ammonia. Reilly unscrewed the top and held it under Pennick's nose. He stirred.

"Okay, boys — hood up."

A few moments later Pennick opened his eyes, but keeping them open was obviously an effort and he blinked rather stupidly about him. Reilly held the salts beneath his nose again and the bound man jerked his head away with alacrity.

"Take a few deep breaths, Mister Pennick. Ye'll soon feel the benefit."

Pennick looked up at the masked men standing round him and with difficulty managed to utter a single croaking word.

"Why ...?"

"All in good time," Reilly answered. "Ye could use some water."

He nodded to Farrell who vanished into the kitchen to draw a glass.

"Nasty stuff, chloroform," he continued. "Your head'll feel like a football for a half-hour or so. No, ye can't get up, I'm afraid. Ye're tied t'the chair. D'ye live alone here? Jus' nod or shake your head." A nod. "Y'expectin' company?" A shake. "Okay, that's fine."

Farrell returned and handed the water to Reilly who held it to Pennick's parched lips.

"Slowly, now," he warned, "or ye'll choke yourself. Had enough?"

A nod. Reilly placed the glass on the polished surface of the dining-table, then pulled up a chair and sat down.

"Right, Mister Pennick, time t'introduce ourselves. We are an active service unit of the Provisional IRA."

Bill Smith was furious.

"What the hell do you mean you've lost them?"

Tango Three's voice crackled over the radio and it was evident that he was none too chuffed about it either.

"When was the last time you took a spin in the country, Bill? These bloody lanes are like the branches on a tree! I stayed well back so they wouldn't clock me. They went round a bend. When I gassed the motor to follow, I found myself at a crossroads. No bloody sign of 'em. One tail just isn't enough for a dog like this. You know that!"

He did. And Thomson did too. But would he bloody listen when reminded?

"All right, Tango. Just stay mobile. You never know, you may get lucky."

"I shouldn't bloody have to, should I? Tango bloody out."

Smith dropped the radio on the bed and stretched the kinks from his back. Frank Hazel, the camera man, shook his head.

"He's right, you know. One car's not enough."

"Do you ever wonder why we bother?" Smith asked. "We've been here nearly a week now. We should have enough identification to maximise resources."

"Maybe after tonight Thomson'll listen?"

"Believe in fairies, do you?"

"I've photographed enough of 'em."

Henry Brooks, the log-man, chuckled from his seat beside the window but he was the only one who did. Smith poured himself a coffee, strong, sweet and black and returned to the bed. Come the morning, he decided, he would get the manpower they needed, even if he had to go over Thomson's head to do it.

"Nine years ago," said Reilly, "ye were part of a team put together by William Tyndall of MI5 t'penetrate the Movement. The operation was designated Gorgon an' the man ye turned was given the codename Perseus. Now this man o'yours has climbed to a very great height indeed. He's been puttin' the finger on all kinds of interestin' things – arms dumps, operations, shipments from Libya – the kind o'stuff which has some very important people pissin' in their wellies. What I want from you is his name."

"And if I told you I didn't know who he was?"

"I'd have t'get nasty, Mister Pennick, an' ye wouldn't like that." He paused. "Let's try again. Let's see if we can't refresh your memory. Ye remember the operation?"

"It was a long time ago."

"But ye remember it?"

"Vaguely."

"Good. Then perhaps ye recall some o'the other men involved?"

"No. I don't. We weren't together very long."

"William Tyndall, ye remember him?" No response. "He's dead, now. It's a pity. I'd have loved t'have a quiet word with him. Inspector Leahy, RUC Special Branch. He's dead too. Up with a bang, as they say, a couple o'years ago. Very nasty. Who else was there? Ah, yes. Major Nigel Barrett, Signals Intelligence. He was a friend o'yours, wasn't he? Funny ye should forget about him, his bein' a friend an' all. An' there was one other. I forget his name. Perhaps ye can remind me No? What was it, now ...? Ah, yes. Peter Wilcox. Ex-captain in the SAS. So, we've identified the brains, now all we need t'find is the hands. But before ye start forgettin' again, let's look at this operation in more detail.

"A decade ago your Intelligence network was a shambles. No one knew what anyone else was up to. No one shared, no one cared. Result: a lot o'touts were turned over into the sunlight, information came to a dead stop – excuse the pun, but a lot o'sources died – an' somethin' had t'be done.

"Your man Tyndall had an idea, an' really it was a pretty good one. Ye take picked men from various units, mix 'em up an' before ye know it ye've a fine wee organisation. Ye've got it locked up nice an' tight, no leaks, it's a winner – a man in on the ground, an SAS contact pipin' the information, brains t'analyse it an' an RUC lifter to act on everythin' ye learned. It was sweet. But o'course the most important man of all was the one ye turned around – the one who ye forced t'betray his people an' his country. Which brings me back t'my original question: who is he? Who is the man codenamed Perseus?"

There was something in Reilly's voice which only added to Pennick's befuddlement. He had a pleasant timbre, spoke in calm and measured tones and his accent lacked the harshness and often tortured vowel-sounds habitually associated with Ulster. Pennick had come across such men before, had worked with them and observed their methods. They were professional interrogators who had been chosen for their physical presence and who did not need to raise their voices to highlight the violence within.

"Who is the man codenamed Perseus?" Reilly repeated.

"It was my job to assess the incoming intelligence," Pennick replied. "I never met the man."

"But you must have known who he was."

It was not a question.

"Why must I? You've just given a wonderful description of the Intelligence mess ten years ago. Too many paid informers were being discovered – too many people knew too much and wouldn't share their information. That was why Gorgon came into being. We were not only part of a new type of operation, we were unique in that we neither met nor knew the identity of the agent we were running. Only Tyndall knew. It was thought to be safer that way – and the fact that he's still in place and kicking you where it hurts proves that it was."

Reilly didn't reply.

"If your intelligence was good enough to uncover the damned operation, I'm surprised you didn't know that we were kept in the dark. How did you find out, anyway? Who told you?

"Even you have your touts."

Pennick nodded. "Its all part o'the game."

His poor imitation of the Ulster accent irritated Gilvarry.

"Shayzus, the bastard's laughin' at us! He fuckin' knows who the tout is!"

Before Reilly could stop him, the youth had sprung forward and punched the bound man hard in the face. The chair overturned and Pennick hit the floor with a crash which knocked him senseless.

"Ye stupid wee bastard!" Reilly cursed. "I told ye not to interfere!"

He slapped Gilvarry and the youth staggered sideways under the impact.

"Help me pick him up," he commanded; and when Pennick was returned to an upright position, he added: "One more stunt like that an' ye're back on the next boat home t'face a court martial. D'ye hear?"

Gilvarry nodded and, picking up the smelling salts, Reilly forced Pennick back into consciousness.

Tango Three pulled in beside a track which led to a farm on the Hampshire/Surrey border.

"Alpha, how long do I have to keep this up?" he asked. "I've been going round in circles for the last half-hour like something in a fairground."

Smith's voice crackled over the radio. "Why don't you count some sheep, or something?"

"I don't think that's very funny."

The clock on the dash read half-past twelve, the moon was high and the clear night sky was flecked with stars. A few moment passed in silence, then the radio crackled back into life.

"All right, Tango, come on home."

Tango Three responded in the affirmative, gunned the engine and slowly drove away.

There was something definitely wrong. Pennick's breathing was laboured, his skin had turned a sickly yellow and glistened with perspiration.

"Mister Pennick ...?"

Still no response.

"What's the matter with him?" Farrell asked.

"How the hell do I know?" Reilly replied.

He emptied the contents of the glass on Pennick's head and the former Intelligence man stirred.

"Mister Pennick, can ye hear me?"

Slowly Pennick opened his eyes. His pupils were dilated and his mouth cracked open as though he were trying to speak.

Reilly turned to Farrell. "Get some more water."

A minute later he was holding the glass to the bound man's lips, urging him to drink.

"C'mon, now, take a sip, take a drink, Mr. Pennick."

Pennick couldn't swallow and the water dribbled from his mouth onto his robe.

"Jimmy, go look in the medicine cabinet — see if there's anythin' there t'fix him up."

"Like what?"

"Shit, I dunno! Tablets, syrup — look for a bottle o'pills, or somethin'!"

Gilvarry obeyed and Reilly tried once more to get Pennick to drink. But it was no use.

This was fast becoming the biggest balls-up he had ever known. There had been no plan — no time in which to prepare — his men were boys as green as spring and one was worse than useless thanks to the collie who lay dead on the rug in the hallway. And if that weren't enough the man they had been sent to interrogate was pegging out and he didn't know why, and he still hadn't got what he had come for.

Gilvarry returned and handed him a safety screw-top bottle of pills. Reilly read the label: *ASPIRIN DISPERSIBLE 75 MG AS DIRECTED.*

"Aspirin ...?"

"S'all I could find."

As he spoke, Gilvarry moved back a step.

With a curse, Reilly spun the cap off and shook a couple into the glass. The water clouded and he wound it into a fizz with his forefinger.

"Drink, ye bastard," he urged. "Don't go friggin' dyin' on me, now."

But as he pressed the glass to Pennick's lips he saw it was already too late. He looked for a pulse. There wasn't one. He checked his eyes with a torch. There was no reaction.

"Is he dead?" Farrell asked.

Reilly nodded. Tearing off his balaclava, Farrell bent over and was violently sick.

"What now?" Gilvarry said.

In reply, Reilly moved across to the mantlepiece where he raked the ornaments to the floor. No one moved, no one spoke; they merely watched in puzzled silence as he did the same to the overburdened bookshelves. Finally, Reilly went into the kitchen where he unlocked the back door and drew back the bolt. Stepping outside, he smashed the glass near the lock, the shards cascading over the white-tiled floor.

"What was all that about?" Gilvarry asked when he returned.

Reilly was still angry. "If ye hadn't belted him we could've laid him back in bed an' dumped the dog in a field. But since ye did, we have t'make it look like he disturbed a break-in."

He bent over the dead man and untied him, stuffing the twine into his pocket and tipping him from the chair to the floor. A final glance and he strode towards the door.

"C'mon," he said. "It's time we was gone. One o'yez lend a hand to Peter."

Five minutes later they were climbing into the White Triumph Estate which Kelly had provided and went tooling back to London.

CHAPTER 15

HARRY Thomson and Frank Davis kept their appointment with the DG at ten o'clock in her office overlooking South Audley Street. Davis had not met the lady boss of MI5 before and found her to be not only charming but also very direct. First, she let Thomson outline Operation Gorgon, interrupting only when she felt a point needed clarifying, then listened as Davis voiced his role in the affair.

"It's hard to believe that a man like William could have been so unprofessional," she said when they had finished. "He should have handed over control of his agent a long time ago. Which brings us to the next question: are we any closer to identifying this man Perseus?"

Thomson shook his head. "I'm afraid not, ma'am. We're still working on it. But unless he contacts Frank, we don't hold out much hope."

"I don't like it, Harry. We've an obligation to look after our people. From what you've said he's provided us with first-class information and apart from the fact that we can't afford to lose such a quality source, he's out there on his own without a safety-net and that's dangerous. I know you didn't create the problem, but the fact remains that you've inherited it. Find him, Harry, and turn him over to Lisburn. At the very least, we owe him that protection."

"Time you were heading back to Ulster, Frank," Thomson said as they waited for the lift. "Get young Jamie to book you on the noon shuttle. Doesn't leave you much time, I know; but needs must when uncertainty drives the train."

"Did Jamie tell you that he wants to try his luck in Ireland?"

"He mentioned it."

"And?"

"Boredom is never a wise ledge to leap from," Thomson replied. "And anyway, he's much to valuable to lose."

Before Davis could reply, the lift arrived and Thomson stepped inside.

"You might as well ring him from here. Get him to meet you at the flat with a car, save you hiring a cab. I know he'll want to say goodbye. Right, I must be going. I've a Directors' meeting in twenty minutes. Take care of yourself, Frank, and don't forget to let me know how you get on."

A cool handshake and Davis was left staring at the polished steel doors of the lift. With a sigh of resignation, he turned and wandered back along the corridor where he asked the DG's secretary for the use of her telephone.

As for Thomson, he had more important things on his mind than the life of an informer. Five minutes after arriving at his office in Curzon Street, Bill Smith had barged in making waves the size of a high-rise. Did he know they had lost the Provo ASU for three- and-half hours? Who the hell knew what they had been up to? Thomson had listened patiently while the irate Watcher verbally destroyed the political and military fabric of a slumbering nation whose protective resources had been so dangerously withheld, then calmly assured him that the said resources would be provided and that they were already on the agenda to be tabled for discussion that very morning, subject of course to the DG's approval.

That had mollified Smith who gave his report and left in a less aggressive manner; but although his concern was well-founded, his attitude was quite unacceptable and Thomson had resolved to discuss the matter with his opposite number in 'A' Branch.

The conference room was on the third floor and, as the lift descended, he tidied his appearance and composed himself for the inevitable — though always outwardly civilised — battle for a larger share of a diminishing budget.

Donal Brady had been wakened at six by the telephone trilling by the bed.

"Hello?"

"Can I speak t'Liam, please?"

A moment passed while the code struck home.

I'm sorry, there's no one by that name here."

"Okay, thanks, sorry to have bothered ye."

"Who was that?" Moira had asked when he had hung up the receiver.

"Wrong number," he had replied, climbing from the bed.

"Where ye goin?"

"Go back t'sleep."

Ten minutes later he had been standing out of the rain in a call-box waiting for the damn thing to ring.

It rang.

"Donal?"

"Jesus, Tim, d'ye know what fuckin' time it is? I thought we agreed ye'd be callin' me at six o'clock in the evenin'!"

"An' so we did, but I thought ye should know that your man Pennick snuffed last night without coughin'."

"What happened?"

Reilly had explained, then waited in silence while Donal digested it.

"Sounds like his heart."

"That's what I thought. Anyway, jus' thought I'd better let ye know."

"Cheers, Tim."

At ten o'clock, he had driven over to Kennedy's with the news. The Chief had cursed the saints to hell and told him bluntly that there were to be no more fuck-ups. Donal had assured him that he would tell the snatch-team to go easy; then he had gone back home into his study where he passed the morning deep in thought.

Tyndall gone, Leahy gone, Barrett out of reach, now Pennick gone. That only left one man who could identify him, the SAS man Peter Wilcox. If Wilcox went the way of all flesh then he would be safe. At least until he managed to arrange for the safe removal of himself and his family.

But how ...?

By lunchtime, he had the solution. Since he couldn't go across the water to do the job himself, he needed to persuade someone to do it for him, one who was not only capable of pulling it off, but who was also unconnected with the Movement. But how to persuade this hypothetical person to undertake the contract ...?

Money was out — he didn't have enough. Besides, when you bought a killing you bought the hand and not the mouth; people talked, and, apart from that, the appearance of someone flinging money around like confetti would only attract unwanted attention and eventual exposure; so a mercenary whacking was out.

Which left a different kind of persuasion, the kind which carried a guarantee of minimal outlay and silence to the grave: blackmail. And Donal only knew one man who was open to such an approach, who was hard enough to do the job and clever enough to succeed.

"God help me, but I'm courtin' the devil himself," he said as he reached for the 'phone. It rang three times. "Sean? It's Donal Brady. I think ye should be meetin' me for lunch ..."

They met in a chip shop along the Falls Road. Donal bought two cups of tea and carried them across to a table in the corner where a short, fair-haired man with a slight build and pale blue eyes awaited him.

It had been a while since Donal had last seen Sean O'Malley and he felt a familiar thrill of fear as he sat down before him. Physically smaller than himself, O'Malley was the most dangerous bastard he had ever met, the kind you stayed away from if you wanted life to be healthy and long. This being so, he almost baulked at carrying out his plan; but then he remembered just what was at stake.

"Been a long time, Sean," he said, winding the sugar in his tea. "How've ye been keepin'?"

"Okay."

"Been workin' at Malloy's, I hear."

Malloy's was an antique restoration firm in White Rock.

O'Malley nodded. "These last six months. Pay's not great, but I like the work. An' you — still at Scampton's?"

"Nah, made redundant three months back. Been livin' off the cheque ever since.

"Tough with a family."

"We make out. Mind you, we got a little put by, ye know. An' when Moira's da passed on last year he left us somethin'."

O'Malley nodded. "Aye, I heard he'd gone."

An Phoblacht had covered the funeral and mourned the passing of a hero, Black Jack Grady, a stalwart of '69 and a notable marksman who had learned his trade in Korea.

"But ye didn't bring me out here for a chinwag, Donal. So how's about ye tellin' me what ye're after?"

"That's one o'the things I always liked about ye," Donal said, returning his cup to its saucer. "No pissin' about, jus' cuttin' straight t'the chase." A pause. "There's a wee job needs doin' across the water."

"Forget it. I'm out of it."

"It wasn't your fault."

"I planted the bomb."

A device he had primed to take out an armoured car had been triggered by a school bus instead. Sixteen children and a nun had been killed and he had been unable to reconcile fifteen years of dedication and inherited idealism with the reality of infanticide. That had been four years ago and he had left the Movement.

"I planted the bomb," he repeated to himself in a quiet tone laced with bitter self-disgust. Donal stayed silent while he considered how best to continue with his plan.

Sean O'Malley was thirty-seven years old and had been raised a Republican in the Ardoyne. Back in '69 when the Troubles had started, he had helped load the Boys' guns as they manned the barricades. At sixteen he had been a runner and at seventeen, following the murder of his brother by the Protestant UVF he had become an ardent member of an active service unit in the Provisional IRA.

He had never risen to command a Brigade: he had always been too much a loner for that. Although he had taken part in many group operations, he had always preferred working alone, a fact which had only been tolerated because of his oft-proven abilities and formidable rate of success. When he had blown up the bus and walked away from violence, there were many in the Movement felt relieved. He was considered unpredictable, uncontrollable and dangerous, a wild card in a game of chance whose loss outweighed his value.

"I'm not askin' ye t'come back t'the Cause," Donal said eventually. "I'm askin' ye t'do a one-off job. A favour, if ye will."

O'Malley looked up. "A favour?"

"T'me."

"What kind of favour?"

"There's someone needs plantin'."

"Forget it."

O'Malley rose and began to walk away when Donal played his trump card.

"By the way, how's Danny?"

Donal had discovered O'Malley's younger brother touting for the Brits and had told no one but Sean who had given him a hiding and sent him to live with an uncle across the border. Had Danny been caught by anyone else he would have been shot for sure and Donal was calling in the debt.

Slowly, O'Malley turned to face him. Did the bastard never blink? Donal felt his heart flutter in his rib cage like a trapped bird. There was no turning back now. It had to be played to the end.

"Be an awful thing if word got out, him bein' so young an' all."

O'Malley said nothing, his blue eyes glacial in his thin pale face.

"But then," Donal continued, "there's no reason why it should ... is there?"

Peter O'Connor was in a bad way. Doctor Patel had given him a tetanus shot and had sewn up the wound in his face.

"I can do nothing more," he said. "But I tell you again he should be in hospital."

Kelly nodded as he peeled five twenty pound notes from his bill fold.

"Aye, but ye see, Doc, he's awful scared o'hospitals. An' I'm sure we can look after him well enough."

He handed the money to the doctor who pocketed it and picked up his bag.

"Well, you must be keeping the wound clean. Change the dressing twice a day and call me if he gets any worse."

"Right. Will do. Will ye have a drink before ye go?"

"No, thank you, I have surgery at five."

"I'll show ye out."

Reilly moved to the bedside. "How're ye feelin'?"

O'Connor tried to smile, but the anaesthetic was beginning to wear off and it hurt, so he nodded instead.

"Good lad. Try an' get some sleep an' I'll be up t'see ye later."

Ever since they had returned from Surrey, Ricky Farrell had been hovering with concern.

"Is he gonna be okay, Mister Reilly?"

"If he gets plenty o'rest."

"Is it okay if I sit with him? I won't disturb him, just ..."

"Sure, son — I'm thinkin' he'll appreciate it."

Farrell smiled nervously and disappeared inside. Reilly closed the door. There was almost something feminine in the youngster's devotion to his friend, like a schoolboy's admiration for a handsome sporting prefect. But O'Connor's disfigurement disqualified him from the role which had been thrust upon him and it reflected well on the younger boy's character that it did not seem to matter.

He went downstairs where he found Kelly pouring a dram beside the liquor cabinet.

"Tim, I was jus' comin' t'call ye. Will ye join me for a drink?"

Reilly shook his head. "Not for me, but I think ye're gonna need one."

Kelly looked nervous. "Why?"

"Well, with Peter out-of-action, we're down t'three an' we're gonna need your help."

Trembling, Kelly downed the dram in one.

CHAPTER 16

SATURDAY morning found Sean O'Malley standing by the entrance of Euston Station. Herds of people bustled about him and the passing traffic swept eddies of foul-tasting grit into the air which made him want to spit. The crossing had been rough, with a foam-capped ocean hurling its malevolent passage in endless waves like a writhe of maddened snakes, and he had been grateful when the rolling boat had finally docked at Liverpool and the world had returned to its level calm and measure.

The arrangements for his short stay had already been taken care of and Brady had also given him a number to call, the number of an arms dealer named Halliday. "Settle in, buy the piece, do the job an' ye'll be troubled no more about Danny," the IRA man had told him. Well, that was true enough. O'Malley was saving a bullet to make sure of it.

Ten minutes passed; then fifteen. Half-an-hour later, a scrawny boy of twenty with carefully combed red hair and nervous blue eyes jogged towards him.

"Mister O'Malley? Name's Cleary. I was told t'meet ye."

"Ye're late."

"The traffic. Ye wouldn't believe the trouble I had gettin' here at all. Can I take your bag?"

They walked to a battered Ford Cortina. Cleary dropped O'Malley's case into the boot, then unlocked the passenger door.

"She might not look like much," he said defensively, "but she goes like a bomb." He ran around to the driver's side and keyed the ignition. "Always starts first time," he said proudly. "Brother-in-law's a mechanic. Has his own garage in Northfields."

He rammed it into gear and the car jerked away towards the traffic and an hour later they pulled in before a house in Connaught Road, West Ealing.

"Place belongs to a fella called Michael Finlay," Cleary explained as he pressed his thumb to the doorbell. "Loves his drink, but he's loyal t'the Cause. Got a wife called Onya, lucky bastard. She's a body on her like a bloody dream an' a wet one at that! I'd love t'give her one."

O'Malley could see why when the door opened and they were faced with a dark-haired woman of thirty with clear features and steady green eyes.

They were shown into a cluttered living room with papers and crayons spread upon the rug before the unlit fire.

"When's Michael back?" Cleary asked.

"Soon," she replied, turning away when a little girl with pigtails raced in through the door. "Have ye finished your lunch?" Her daughter nodded, eyes fixed shyly on the company. "All of it?" Another nod.

"I'd love some tea," said Cleary.

Five minutes later she returned with a tray of tea and Cleary leered as she bent to place it on the coffee-table before them. If she knew the effect she had, she gave no sign of it. O'Malley doubted if she even cared.

"Michael," said Cleary rising when Onya's husband came in a few minutes later, "I'd like ye t'meet Sean O'Malley."

Finlay, a big man stained with brick dust and sweat, dumped his tool bag on the floor inside the living room doorway and nodded.

"Best be puttin' the dinner on," he said to his wife. "We don't want our guest thinkin' we've no hospitality."

Onya withdrew and Cleary clapped and rubbed his hands with exaggerated decision.

"Right, well I'll be off. Ye have my number, Mister O'Malley. If ye need anythin', jus' gimme a call. So long."

Finlay followed him out and O'Malley found himself alone in a room in a house where he did not feel welcome.

It was Mrs. Jarvis who found him. She explained to the police how she had let herself in and first discovered the collie and then its master lying dead upon the floor. In all her years of cleaning house she had never been so shocked. And the mess! Well, poor Mister Pennick had obviously heard them breaking in – had they seen the state of the back door? All that glass – oh, it was horrible! And why on earth had they had to kill him, him being such a nice man and all ...

Detective Inspector Matthews watched the scenes-of-crime officer at work. There were no prints – the burglars had obviously been wearing gloves – and on the face of it there were too few clues to satisfy enquiries. There was blood in the bathroom and the medicine cupboard above the sink had been swept clean of its contents. Pills, potions, plasters and salves lay haphazardly on the carpeted floor and a bottle of milk of magnesia had smashed into the crescent-shaped bath.

A dead man in the living room and blood on the bathroom floor ... had the burglars panicked? Had they dragged him in and tried to fix him up, failed and then returned him to the living room where he had died?

Or had one of them been injured? By the dog perhaps? If so, where was the detritus, the evidence of this hurried ministration?

Something didn't sit right which persuaded the policeman that all was not as it seemed. It could have been a burglary attempt, for everything looked consistent with the thieves having been disturbed at work. But if they had been cool enough to minister to an injury, why leave empty-handed? Had they left empty-handed? The TV, stack-system stereo and VCR were still in place. The dead man's wallet containing plastic cards and sixty pound in notes had been left untouched in his jacket pocket hanging on the back of a dining-table chair. If they hadn't been interested in these then what had they been after? Or was he letting his imagination get the better of him?

When SOCO had finished and the bodies were removed, Matthews let his men prowl with less care. The lie of some of the objects on the floor were consistent with their having been swept with some force from the mantlepiece, and that was suspicious enough in that it implied a considered action – although he had to admit it could have been done in a struggle or a fit of temper; but his instincts told him otherwise. And why rake books from the shelves unless they thought they were concealing something? And if so, what ...?

No, it just didn't sit right. Matthews had seen enough burglaries to believe that the mess was merely camouflage to hide the true intention of whoever it was who had broken in; but as to what the true intention was, he could not even begin to guess – at least until he knew a whole lot more about the man who had been killed.

For the second time that week Emily Baker grew tired of looking at the clock upon the living room wall as she knew with bitter certainty that Patrick Kelly would not be coming. Eight o'clock he had said – eight o'clock and then a night of wine and dancing which would only end when the sun rose – but it was after nine now and she knew he was not coming.

God, what a fool she was, she thought, as she pulled the clip-on turquoise rings from her ears and dropped them on the low pine coffee-table before her. Kelly didn't want her, didn't love her, didn't need her; he promised her the world and she was stupid enough to believe him, which was why she was sat there in a new low-cut black mock-silk evening dress and hair newly-permed, the total expense of which was close to a whole week's pay, extravagance she would never had considered for herself alone.

She turned the television on and, kicking off her stiletto-heeled shoes, returned to the couch where she drew her feet up under her. On BBC 1 was the end of a film – The Great Gatsby, the remake starring Robert

Redford and Mia Farrow – but she paid it cursory heed, her thought not unnaturally being centred on the painful predicament in which she found herself, that of being a woman in love with a man who was unworthy of her and of being stood-up by him for the second time that week; and then came the news and she got up and made herself a cup of instant coffee and a thin-sliced turkey sandwich on a bed of salt.

"And finally, some news just in ..." said the telecaster, reading from a sheet which had been handed to him; and Emily paused with the sandwich halfway to her mouth as she heard about the death of Alan Pennick, the popular historian. She put down the plate and, reaching for the remote-control handset, turned up the volume. "Although little is known at present, police are treating his death as suspicious. We'll have more on this item in our bulletin at midnight."

She rose and switched off the set and returned to the couch in a daze. Alan Pennick had been one of the men on the list she had given to Kelly. A wave of cold apprehension swept over her and she tried to believe it was merely a coincidence, but the report had said that the police were treating his death as suspicious. Could Kelly have been involved? Had he ...?" No, it was impossible, he would never have done such a thing. But the fact remained that Pennick was dead and the sting of doubt was pricking at her mind. She finished her coffee and, binning the sandwich, climbed the stairs uneasily to bed.

Sean O'Malley also went to bed early that night. He had been for a drink in the Prince Arthur and had watched with disgust as Michael Finlay became drunk. The evening would only have one outcome and he had not been in the mood for a fight; besides, he had been a long day travelling and was ready for a good night's sleep.

He returned to find Onya putting Kathie to bed. She saw him but did not return his smile and, wordlessly, he went to the room which they had set aside for him, a small box-room – more of a store cupboard, really – with a camp bed tucked in tight behind the door. As he undressed, he thought of what had brought him to England, of his brother and the man who had used him as a lever; of how he had been forced back into a life he had foresaken for the purpose of killing a stranger for a reason which was never volunteered. Earlier that evening he had telephoned the number Brady had given him and had arranged to meet the arms dealer, Halliday, at a piece of wasteground bordering a housing estate in Acton. That would take care of the hardware. The next step was more difficult. He had to identify the target, a man called Peter Wilcox, draw his gun and calmly take his life. Then he had to walk away as if he were merely out for a stroll, then leave behind him this alien shore as free of suspicion as he had entered it.

A young English poet who had died in the Second World War, a man called Douglas, had written a poem on the ease with which one man could take the life of another. O'Malley had only come upon it when he had quit the IRA and had felt, by instinct, cousined to the thoughts set out therein. Although he had read the poem many times, he had no gift for remembering verse like so many of his countrymen; but one line had adhered: 'How easy it is to make a ghost'. Too damned easy he thought, turning out the light and clambering into bed.

He didn't sleep well, what with Finlay's drunken and abusive return and the ghost of a violent past rising up with renewed determination to trouble him. It was almost two o'clock before he finally succumbed and he wakened, red-eyed, four hours later, unable to sleep any more.

So he rose and quietly went downstairs into the kitchen where he made himself a cup of tea and two slices of richly-buttered toast. An hour later he was joined by Onya. She and Kathie were going to church and when they had gone he telephoned Cleary.

"Jaysus, what time is it?" the youth demanded tiredly.

"Time t'go t'work," O'Malley replied. "Pick me up in an hour."

Without waiting for a reply, he hung up and went back upstairs to get washed and, an hour later, Cleary arrived.

CHAPTER 17

WHAT was it like?" Cleary asked.

O'Malley remembered how West Belfast had erupted in a storm of gunshots and sectarian chanting, how the darkening streets had been lit by bonfires and the way the ground had trembled beneath the weight of the patrolling Shorland armoured cars.

"It was noisy."

"Must've been exciting, though?"

He rembered seeing a Proddie shot as he was preparing to hurl a petrol bomb at the retreating Catholic crowd. It had exploded beneath him as he fell.

"They say ye were a hero."

"I was a child."

Big Jim Shaughnessy had charged up Dover Street like the devil himself, skilfully dodging the flying bricks and dustbin lids. The bingo hall was on fire, throwing flickering light upon the faces of the Protestants as they scattered before him. The noise had been indescribable, but O'Malley had still heard the pistol shot which sent Shaughnessy to the ground.

"They say the Big Man would've died if it hadn't been for you."

O'Malley had raced towards the mobile barricade in time to see a man reload his pistol and point it at Shaughnessy as he struggled to his feet. The Big Man's own revolver had lain at his side. O'Malley had snatched it up and fired without aiming and had seen the Proddie gunman fall, his face a mask of twisted disbelief. Then he had passed out and remembered no more until he had woken up in the front room of an unfamiliar house in the daylight to find Big Jim standing over him with his arm in a sling and a smile on his face.

Thirteen years old when he had killed his first man and the time for killing was not yet over ...

"I wonder what's takin' your man so long?" Cleary asked. "We've been sat here nearly half-an-hour, already."

In the wing mirror O'Malley saw a blue Mercedes turn into the street and crawl along the wasteground towards them. It had already passed by twice before.

"Wait here," he said and climbed out into the open. The driver of the

Mercedes cut the engine and the gorilla in the front passenger seat got out, his eyes never leaving O'Malley and opened the back door.

"Grady?" a voice asked. O'Malley nodded and a dark-skinned man oozed from the car, all grease and gold. "Name's Halliday," he said, extending a cashmere arm. "You said you could use a little weight?"

He flicked his fingers and gorilla popped the boot. It was filled with weaponry, ranging from the ever-popular Armalite to the Czech-designed AK47 assault rifle and a modest assortment of handguns. O'Malley stepped forward and picked out a 9mm Beretta.

"Nice little number," Halliday said. "Rarely jams, it's accurate and easily concealed."

O'Malley put it back and chose a Walther PP Automatic. He pulled back the slide and gazed down the ejection port, then with his thumb released the hammer.

".32 calibre," Halliday said. "Eight shot, double-action. Light but deadly."

"I'll take it."

"You'll want a couple of spare clips?"

O'Malley nodded.

"Then all we need discuss is the price."

"Ye said three hundred on the 'phone."

"Must have been a fault on the line. I said five. Four-fifty for the piece, another fifty for the clips and ammo."

O'Malley sensed gorilla moving behind him. "Three hundred, or ye can stuff it."

"Oh, dear. I had hoped you'd be reasonable."

The Irishman sensed the danger as it happened and pivoted away, his right elbow shooting back catching gorilla in the midriff. Still turning, he followed up with a rising kick to the testicles and, as gorilla began to fold, smashed his knee into his face, his nose exploding into a bloody pulp as the cartilage disintegrated.

Halliday watched his protection crumple to the ground like used tissue, then began to back away. O'Malley turned and stared at the arms dealer, his blue eyes blazing.

"Was it worth it?" he asked.

"Keep away from me! I'm warning you!"

But O'Malley did not keep away. He took a step forward.

Halliday was shaking "Tanner!"

His driver did not move, staying frozen behind the wheel.

"All right!" Halliday cried. "Three hundred!"

O'Malley took another step towards him. "How much?"

"Nothing ... Just don't hurt me ..."

Cleary had got out of the car by now and was staring in fascination at gorilla lying unconscious on the ground.

Halliday sank to his knees. "Please ..."

O'Malley looked down at him with contempt. "The clips."

"In-in the tool box."

He nodded to Cleary who walked to the boot, returning with a bundle of clips held together by an elastic band. O'Malley selected three then ordered Cleary back to the car.

"What are you going to do with me?" Halliday whimpered.

O'Malley rammed a clip into the butt of the Walther and jacked a round into the breech.

"No ... You can't ...!"

He felt the muzzle of the loaded pistol press into the nape of his neck.

"Goodbye, Mister Halliday," O'Malley said softly.

The arms dealer shut his eyes tight and waited for the shot which never came. What seemed like an eternity later, he heard an engine start and opened his eyes to find the Irishmen driving away. He climbed unsteadily to his feet, his fouled trousers clinging to his legs, and stumbled after them, fists pounding the air.

"Grady ... You dirty Mick bastard!" he cried, while behind him gorilla stirred painfully as he regained consciousness.

Harry Thomson was sitting in the armchair by the window in his small Hammersmith flat with his eyes closed and his senses dead to all but the music swelling from the hi-fi in the corner. He had always loved classical music and Mozart's Requiem was one of his favourites and the fact that the young composer had been dying when he wrote it seemed to give it a special power, a piquancy which stirred his emotions like no other piece could.

He sat quite still but for the occasional movement when he went to take a sip from the brandy glass held loosely in his left hand or to relight his Sunday pipe, a Peterson with a rich brown bowl and a curved stem. The fragrant mixture of tobaccos curled into a cloud which revolved beneath the low stained ceiling, gradually moving like a mist through the living room door into the hallway where it flattened and dispersed in the draught from the open kitchen window.

Although it was Sunday and he wasn't going into the office, Thomson was wearing a tie. It was something his father had always done and, although the son wasn't going to church, it was a habit he had never felt like breaking, for in some tenuous way it was a link to the past. Apart from that, he was an orderly, tidy man; routines were important for you always knew where you were. By doing things in a particular way at a particular time you pressed some order into the day. Work had its routines, so why should home be any different?

Sundays had a pattern he had woven over many years. Rising at ten, he would cook a light breakfast and then go out for a walk to buy the paper. At two o'clock, he would have a light lunch (a tossed salad with Thousand Isle dressing), spend the afternoon with his pipe and a selection of his favourite music; and at six o'clock he would prepare the evening meal, wash the dishes and end the day in front of the television, finally going to bed at half-past ten. It was a routine he was comfortable with, he found it reassuring; and but for a crisis which would drive him back to the office, Sunday was his day.

The telephone rang. At first he tried to ignore it, but its shrill persistent clamour grated harshly on an ear attuned to Mozart. He cursed and, turning down the volume of the music, slippered out into the hallway where he snatched up the receiver.

"Hello?"

"I'm sorry to bother you at home, sir."

"Yes, Jamie — what is it?"

"Mrs. Tyndall, sir, she says she needs to see you. I told her you'd be back in the office tomorrow, but she said it couldn't wait, that she had to see you now."

"All right. You'd better give me her number."

Daniels did and Thomson hung up and dialled.

"Monica? Harry. What can I do for you?"

"It's more what I can do for you," she replied. "When Billy died, one of your spooks packed his things up and brought them over — you know, personal bits and bobs. I'd forgotten all about it; but this morning, Penny was having a mooch about in the attic and she came across the box and found a book called Classic Myth and Legend by A.R. Hope-Moncrieff and I was wondering whether it could be the book you were looking for?"

Thomson sighed — another Sunday gone west.

"All right, Monica; I'll be round within the hour. And Monica —"

"Mmm?"

"Thanks."

He hung up and called Daniels ordering him to requisition a car, to collect the last message from Perseus and to pick him up. Then he went into the kitchen where he fixed himself a sandwich and a cup of black coffee laced with brandy.

An hour later they were sitting in the library at Chardonay, Daniels calling out the code and Thomson matching it to the book. To Thomson's relief the journey hadn't been wasted and he felt a tight excitement as the message was gradually rendered en claire.

When they had done he read it through, then passed it to Daniels whose youthful face grew serious.

"Is he in trouble, your man?" Monica asked.

Thomson nodded. "Yes, and I'm afraid he's not alone."

They thanked her and departed on their journey back to Curzon Street. Frank Davis had to be apprised of the urgency of Perseus's appeal for rescue; but more importantly, in Thomson's view, the surviving members of the Gorgon team had to be warned and arrangements made with Special Branch for their protection.

While the men from MI5 were thus engaged, O'Malley and Cleary were sitting parked across the road from Wilcox's flat. At six o'clock the former SAS man returned and keyed himself indoors. Close behind him, a blue BMW containing four men stopped. One of them got out, taking up a position of observation, and then the car drove away.

"Would ye look at that, now," O'Malley breathed. It was fast becoming an interesting day.

CHAPTER 18

PETER Wilcox flicked around the channels then hit the standby. He never seemed to have the time for watching telly these days and when he did flop down before the box he usually fell asleep, bored as he was by much of the rubbish plugged as popular entertainment.

The telephone rang. He picked it up.

"Mister Wilcox? Jamie Daniels. Will you be in this evening? Only something's come up — something important — and I think we ought to talk."

It had been a long day and Wilcox was tired, but he consented to the MI5 man's request; and having agreed to drop round at eight Daniels hung up and Wilcox made a coffee.

At seven-fifty the doorbell rang. Wilcox lifted the entry-phone and, without checking the identity of the caller, pressed the door-release buzzer. A few moments later, he heard footsteps on the stairs and opened his front door fully intending to take Daniels to task for arriving too early which explained the lag in his reactions; for instead of Daniels he found himself staring into the cold blue eyes of a hooded man, a man who moved quicker than he did slamming a front kick into his solar plexus which knocked the wind from his lungs and sent him flying back into the wall.

Two other hooded men ran in behind the first who followed up the attack with a vicious stamp at Wilcox's head. Wilcox who had seen it coming, twisted desperately aside and flicked his left foot at the man's supporting knee. A grunt of pain and his assailant threw an arm against the wall to steady himself. Still moving, Wilcox tried to rise, but one of the others leapt forward and kicked him hard in the ribs. Then he curled up tight to protect himself from the barrage of blows which followed.

The beating sapped him of the strength to resist and he was unable to prevent the men from unfolding him onto his back. Then he saw the one with cold blue eyes remove a cotton pad from his pocket and a jar of liquid. Strong hands gripped his head and held it still and then he was breathing through the pad, drawing the vapour deep into his lungs as a fist slammed into his belly. The blow was repeated and the pain began to recede as he gratefully surrendered to the chloroform, spinning into the darkness as it overcame his senses.

When he came to he felt nauseous. It felt like he had been out for days; his head was throbbing and his throat felt dry. He tried to open his eyes, but there was something preventing him from doing so. He was also tightly bound to a chair.

"He's comin' round," said a voice.

"Remove the blindfold," said another.

Wilcox felt a tugging at the back of his head and as the blindfold fell away he was dazzled by a sharp light stabbing into his eyes. Squinting, he could just make out the blurred outlines of two figures standing before him.

"Where am I?" he croaked.

"Out in the middle o'bloody nowhere, so if ye're thinkin' o'shoutin' for help I wouldn't bother 'cause no one'll hear ye."

Irish. Wilcox blinked into the light. "Isn't this where I'm supposed to say you'll never get away with this?"

Suddenly, a fist drilled into his kidneys betraying the presence of a man in position behind him, and Wilcox, keeling forward under the violence of the blow, vomited on the floor.

"Now there are two ways we can do this," blue eyes said, "the hard way or the easy way. I prefer the easy way meself, but these other boys, well – they're new at this game. They don't know what real pain's like."

"And I bet they're just dying to find out," Wilcox replied, wheezing as he fought to outdistance the pain in the race to catch his breath.

"So ye see it's really up to you. But I'd prefer it if ye see some sense an' co-operate."

"I've always been a sensible man."

"Good." Blue eyes pulled up a chair and, readjusting the position of the light, outlined Operation Gorgon.

"You're very well informed," Wilcox said, feeling his pain withdrawing. "But I fail to see why you've taken me. You probably know more than I do."

"It's a funny thing," blue eyes said, "but I'm disinclined to agree with ye. Ye're the only one who had direct contact with the man ye codenamed Perseus; an' as much as I'd like t'believe ye're just another ignorant lackey o'British Imperialism I can't, so the sooner ye tell me who the bastard is the sooner ye can go."

Wilcox chuckled. He knew he was never going to leave this place alive. SAS men, retired or otherwise, were prestige targets for the Provo trophy-room; and although he was afraid, he felt strangely resigned to the inevitable. But one thing was for sure – he would not give up without a fight. If he was going to die he would make it hard for the bastards; at least that way it would be quick and, thus resolved, he began to work on his bonds.

"And if I told you I don't know who he is?"

"Don't play games with your life, Mister Wilcox. I'm warnin' ye." Blue eyes paused. "Now, let's try again. Give me the name o'the man code-named Perseus."

"I don't know," Wilcox truthfully replied and felt his skull explode into coloured fragments as he was struck from behind.

"The name!"

When Wilcox didn't reply, the short figure standing beside blue eyes leapt forward and drove a boot into his solar plexus.

"We're wastin' time," said the man behind him. "Let's jus' blow his soddin' head off an' get out o'here!"

Through his pain, Wilcox heard them arguing. Their voices sounded so far away. He tried to listen to what they were saying — to understand what was happening — but it all seemed so disjointed and unreal and he soon felt himself slipping back into unconsciousness.

Onya turned the television off and looked at Katie.

"Come on, you. Time for bed."

"Oh, Mom ..."

"Never mind 'Oh Mom'. Jus' do as ye're told."

Katie sighed and made her way to the door.

"Say goodnight t'Mister O'Malley."

"G'night, Mister O'Malley."

"Sleep tight, now."

He watched them go and smiled and a few minutes later Onya returned.

"Sorry t'bother ye, Mister O'Malley."

"Sean," he corrected.

"It's Katie. She wants ye t'read her a bedtime story."

"Does she now?"

"I wouldn't ask, but it's murder gettin' her off t'sleep as it is. Would you mind?"

He found Katie lying in a bed that was too big for her, the covers pulled right up to her chin. On the bedside table beside the lamp was a well-thumbed volume of fairy stories. He picked it up.

"Which one would ye like?" he asked.

"The one about the frog," she whispered.

He found the story, then sat on the bed beside her.

"Once upon a time ..." he began.

When she had fallen asleep he turned out the light and, closing the door softly behind him, joined Onya on the landing.

"I wish Michael'd read t'her," she said. "He used to. He'd come in early an' we'd spend the whole night talkin'."

O'Malley studied her in the dim light. She was a beautiful woman, with fine bones and a full figure hidden beneath the shapeless clothes.

"What about?"

She laughed, a short self-conscious sound that stroked his belly with its warmth.

"Oh, ye know, how rich he was gonna make us. How Katie'd go to a posh school where they'd teach her t'be clever. He was always dreamin'."

Suddenly, O'Malley took her in his arms and kissed her. She started to struggle, to pull away, but he held on tight and she gradually relented. His hands wandered from her arms to her breasts and neck and then she pulled away from him. "Not here," she whispered and, taking his hand, she led him along the narrow landing to her bedroom.

They made love twice: first, with a hunger which seemed impossible to satiate, and finally with a slow deliberateness, enjoying the sensation, trying to prolong it, and then they slept. Onya wakened to find O'Malley standing by the window, his shirt unbuttoned and a cigarette burning in his mouth.

"What're ye thinkin' about?" she asked. And when he didn't reply she climbed naked from the bed and joined him at the window. "Mister O'Malley ...?"

"For God's sake, colleen, I think ye know me well enough by now t'call me by me first name."

The colour mounted to her cheeks and she smiled with embarrassment. "Sean."

"That's better," he said, drawing her towards him. They kissed and then he picked her up and carried her back to the bed.

Michael Finlay had been in another fight. His lip was bleeding and he was by far the worse for drink. As he staggered into the street, he stumbled and, steadying himself against a car, caught sight of O'Malley framed in his bedroom window.

At first he couldn't believe what he was seeing; but when he saw his wife appear beside O'Malley and he saw them embrace his facial expression shifted from disbelief to anguish and finally set into a cruel mask of cold hard anger.

Sobering fast, he bitterly turned and went back the way he had come. The bastard would pay — he'd see him in hell! He broke into a run and turned the corner.

The telephone rang. Onya got up and answered it.

"Sean ...? It's for you."

O'Malley climbed from the bed, pulled his trousers on and went downstairs into the hallway where she handed him the receiver.

"Mister O'Malley?" It was Cleary. "There's somethin' funny goin' on. I think ye'd better get down here right away ..."

They watched the men carry Wilcox from his flat to the waiting BMW. O'Malley nodded, Cleary gunned the engine and they took off in pursuit.

The journey into Chiswick lasted little more than ten minutes. There wasn't much traffic on the roads and O'Malley had to keep on warning Cleary to maintain a reasonable distance. They drove across an intersection and along a winding road running parallel with the river. There were hardly any street-lights and those that were working cast an eerie yellow glow upon the pitted road.

They soon found themselves approaching a storage facility. The BMW stopped and O'Malley ordered Cleary to cut the lights and engine. They saw a man jump out of the BMW and unlock the gates and when the car had driven through he replaced the padlock and chain, jumped back in and the car continued for another forty yards, stopping before a line of warehouses standing out like mountain crags against the darkening sky.

A moment later the loading area was bathed in fluorescent light as the sliding door to one of the storage buildings was opened. The BMW drove inside and then the light was extinguished.

"What now?" Cleary asked.

O'Malley took the Walther from his pocket and checked the clip.

"I was afraid of that."

Feeling his belly tighten uncomfortably, Cleary followed O'Malley across the road towards the locked gates of the perimeter fence. In a nearby warehouse, one of the Watchers picked up his radio.

"Alpha, this is Bravo."

"Go ahead, Bravo."

"Target One's paying us a night-time visit."

"Roger, Bravo, keep us informed."

Bravo tossed the radio back upon the desk and, with a cursory glance at the darkened loading area, resumed his perusal of the centrefold before him, missing the two crouching figures loping across the tarmac.

But for the BMW and a pile of crates stacked in the corner, the warehouse was virtually empty. Through the cracked and grimy window they saw Wilcox tied to a chair and bathed in the light from an anglepoise lamp clamped to a cheap wooden table. There were three men with him, two in front concealed by the glare of the light and one standing behind. Each man wore a balaclava.

O'Malley could hear voices raised in anger, but the words were indistinct. He had to get closer. Cleary winced as he saw one of them step forward and kick Wilcox in the solar plexus, then followed O'Malley to the small office attached to the rear of the main structure.

Fortunately, the construction was weathered and O'Malley had little trouble forcing entry. They moved inside and, closing the door quietly behind them, found themselves standing in the centre of a box-shaped office containing two desks, a filing cabinet, and a pile of clumsily stacked invoices in the corner beside the interior doorway. What they did not see was the old tin kettle perched haphazardly on the edge of the nearest desk. Cleary moved closer to O'Malley, his hand outstretched in the darkness, and sent it clattering to the floor.

The men in the warehouse froze. The one who was seated, Tim Reilly, turned to the smaller man beside him.

"Ricky, go check it out."

Ricky Farrell took a Webley revolver from his pocket and made his way to the office.

O'Malley had stopped the kettle with his foot the second it had hit the floor.

"Quick!" he hissed and Cleary followed him across the office where they positioned themselves either side of the doorway.

A few seconds later they heard footsteps padding towards them. Then the door handle turned. When Farrell entered, O'Malley leapt out and, disarming him with impressive speed, clasped his hand across the youth's mouth and lowered him gently to the floor, his forearm pressing down on his windpipe.

Cleary closed the door and watched as Farrell's thrashing grew weaker and less determined, until finally the struggling stopped altogether.

"Is he dead?"

O'Malley shook his head. "Help me get him t'the chair."

Cleary pulled the swivel chair out from under the desk and helped O'Malley tie him to it with a ball of waxed twine he had found on the floor beside the invoices.

O'Malley removed the balaclava and they found themselves staring at the smooth face of a boy of about seventeen.

"Know him?" O'Malley asked.

Cleary shook his head. "What now?"

O'Malley handed him the youth's revolver. "Better hang on to this," he said.

"What're you gonna do?"

"Somethin' bloody foolish," O'Malley replied.

Wilcox was still unconscious. The leader was talking quietly to the other man when O'Malley entered wearing Ricky's coat and balaclava.

"All right?" Reilly asked.

O'Malley nodded.

"Okay, Jimmy," he said.

From his pocket, the man behind Wilcox removed a small glass phial which he crushed beneath the unconscious man's nose. Wilcox came to, blinking in the harsh light, wincing as the pain returned.

"Ye're bein' foolish," Reilly said in reasonable tones. "Where's the sense in takin' a hidin' for a bastard tout ye owe nothin' to? D'ye think he'd protect you?"

Wilcox didn't reply.

"Use your brain, man. Jus' tell us who the tout is an' we'll let ye crawl away. Give us the name o'the man codenamed Perseus, the man ye helped t'turn."

Again, Wilcox made no reply. His perception was fragmented and he couldn't glue it back together.

"I told ye," Jimmy growled. "It's a waste o'time! Let's jus' top the bastard an' get out o'here!"

The leader started to bark a warning, but Jimmy had already drawn his gun. O'Malley didn't know he was following a plan which Reilly had evolved to break Wilcox down, didn't know if he planned to use it and couldn't take the chance. There was something going on here — something which he did not understand — and, pulling the Walther from his pocket, he shot Gilvarry neatly between the eyes.

The rest happened very quickly. Reilly had already drawn his weapon and O'Malley was forced to roll away and come up shooting. He hit him twice — once in the shoulder and once in the head, the bullet ripping the flesh from his cheekbone, and the light went out as he fell across the table. In the moonlight, O'Malley saw him scuttling towards the window. He raised his pistol and prepared to fire another round, when Cleary came bounding in waving the captured Webley.

"What the fuck's goin' on?" he cried.

"Get down!" O'Malley yelled and Cleary flung himself to the floor, a bullet carving into the woodwork behind him.

O'Malley swung back as he heard the glass in the window smash. He saw a figure silhouetted briefly in the moonlight and snapped off three more shots, cursing as they missed allowing Reilly to hurl himself through the jagged frame and disappear into the darkness.

O'Malley shoved the Walther back into his pocket and turned to find Cleary poised on all fours, the Webley held tight in his right fist and his eyes wide open in shocked disbelief as he stared at the dead man before him.

"Put that thing away," O'Malley ordered, removing his balaclava. "An' give me a hand."

Cleary didn't move.

"Now!"

Slowly, the youth obeyed. He climbed unsteadily to his feet and, pushing the revolver down the waistband of his trousers, helped return Wilcox, who had been knocked over when Jimmy had fallen, to a sitting position.

"Jesus!" said Cleary, looking at the body and the pool of blood before him. "Jesus!"

"Never mind your cursin'," O'Malley said. "See if the keys are in the car."

Cleary sprinted across and checked. "They are!"

"Don't jus' stand there gapin'. Get the bloody thing started!"

While Cleary turned the engine over, O'Malley opened the door. Then he ran back to the car and jumped inside.

"Move!"

Cleary punched the accelerator and the car jerked, almost stalled, then shot out into the loading area and crashed out through the gates. Bravo, who had heard the shots, snatched up his radio and called for immediate assistance and watched impotently as the BMW sailed out into the night and vanished down the approach road.

They dumped the BMW and clambered into Cleary's car.

"Where to?" Cleary asked. "Finlay's?"

O'Malley nodded and a quarter-of-an-hour later they stopped short of Connaught Road. Three police cars were parked outside the safehouse. In the street, Finlay was talking with a couple of plainclothes officers. A moment later, a uniformed constable appeared with O'Malley' suitcase.

"Bastard!" Cleary said. "He's bloody shopped ye!"

"Let's get out o'here," O'Malley replied, his face an expressionless mask.

Cleary put the car into reverse and they headed back down to the Uxbridge Road.

"Why would he do a thing like that? I thought he was straight!"

O'Malley didn't know but he could guess. In the window he had seen Onya looking out. Although he couldn't be sure he thought he had seen her face all puffed and swollen.

"Bastard!" Cleary cried, then thumped the steering wheel.

"We'll have t'ditch the car," O'Malley said. "Michael's seen it. Which means the police'll have a description."

"Ye don't seem surprised," Cleary said. "If I were you I'd be hoppin' bloody mad!"

"My old Da had a sayin' he was rather fond of," O'Malley replied. "Why get mad when ye can get even."

He had spoken softly and when Cleary looked across and saw his face he thanked God he wasn't in Finlay's shoes.

CHAPTER 19

HELL and bloody damnation!" Thomson muttered, staring at the carnage in the warehouse. Daniels had already prepped him with the details he had managed to discover — rather scant details considering Wilcox's battered recollection — and although they now knew why the Provo ASU had come to the mainland, another part had been added to the equation which made things more puzzling than ever: the timely intervention and identity of the mysterious bloody rescuer.

He watched the crew of an ambulance help Wilcox, who was draped with a bright red blanket, into the back of their wagon, then signalled to Daniels, who was speaking to a Special Branch Inspector, to join him.

"Is he going to be all right?"

Daniels shrugged. "Don't see why not. He's been given a bit of a hiding and he's suffering from shock, but apart from that he's fine. Not like him," he added, jerking his thumb at Gilvarry's corpse which lay, uncovered, where it had fallen.

"Save your sympathy," Thomson replied, unmoved. "He got what he deserved. As will ..."

"Farrell, sir. Richard Farrell."

"When we've had a little chat."

Special Branch had found the young Provisional tugging with fear at the twine which bound him to the chair. He was now sitting under guard and handcuffed in the back of an unmarked SB car which would shortly take him to the high-security nick in Paddington Green. One of his eyes was closed and discoloured with bruising and his lips were split and crusted with blood. Apparently he had tried to resist arrest. Thomson knew it wasn't true; but what the hell — he *was* a bloody terrorist.

"All set, sir?"

The SB man, a short, thickset Scot named McKewan, called from the car.

Thomson waved. "Wrap it up tight, Jamie. Spin the Press a tale."

Daniels gave a wry grimace. "You want a Jack Higgins job or a Gerald Seymour?"

"You can give them Hans Christian bloody Anderson for all I care, just get it done!"

"Yes, sir."

Thomson bowled off in the car for Paddington Green and Daniels set his mind to dreaming up a story suitable for release.

Patrick Kelly and Seamie had spent the evening working on one of his houses. Driving back from Hammersmith, it was nearly eleven when they reached Gordon Road. Kelly was looking forward to a long hot bath, a couple of drinks and a good night's sleep, when Seamie suddenly jumped on the brakes.

"Jesus, Mary an' Joseph!"

"Wha—?" Kelly began to say, alarmed by the emergency stop; and then he stared in disbelief at the police cars ranged before his house. "Sweet mother o'God!"

He didn't need to tell Seamie to get them the hell out of there. Seamie was already reversing at speed towards Haven Green, throwing the car blindly round the corner and narrowly missing an estate car locked into the one-way system, its horn blaring angrily as it swerved and mounted the pavement; and then they were flying past the intersection, tyres squealing as they hedged the roundabout, gunning left by the Berni Inn and on to the Uxbridge Road.

Half-an-hour later they were back in Hammersmith, parking in Lakeside Road before the house they were remodelling. Seamie cut the engine, his face was drawn and his hands were trembling as he took a cigarette from the pack on the dash and lighted it.

"What the fuck's happenin', Paddy?"

"How the fuck do I know?"

Kelly's previous mood of lazy gaiety had been crushed by a sobering fear and his only thoughts were that Reilly had failed, had been taken and had shopped him.

They left the car and hurried up the path. In the pale moonlight, the three-storeyed house he had picked up for a third of its market-value because of fire-damage had taken on a threatening aspect. Its broad bay windows stared out into the darkness like something from a horror film and its very size imposed itself on his vulnerable imagination.

He reached into his pocket. "Shit!"

"What?"

"The keys. I left 'em in the glove-box."

Seamie went back to the car to fetch them and Kelly, waiting by the entrance to the porch, heard something moving within.

"Who's there ...?" he demanded, his voice cracking fearfully up the scale.

A groan. Cautiously, he stepped forward and peered inside the weathered arch. It was Tim Reilly bleeding like a stuck fowl and eyes closed tight against the pain.

"Sweet Christ!"

The fallback plan. If anything went wrong they had decided to run to Lakeside Road. Seamie returned.

"Paddy, what the—"

"Shut up!" Kelly replied. "An' help me get him inside." And when Seamie didn't move: "Don't jus' stand there! Get that bloody door open!"

"Your name is Richard Francis Farrell," Thomson said, reading from a slim file he had taken from his briefcase. "You were born on the twenty-seventh of February, 1976, in West Belfast. You have two brothers, Seamus and Daniel, and a sister, Maureen, who is currently serving a fifteen-year prison sentence for the attempted murder of an off-duty policeman and the illegal possession of an unlicensed firearm. Your father — Michael Patrick Farrell — was a motor mechanic and was killed—"

"Murdered!"

"—by unidentified members of the Ulster Volunteer Force. And your mother, Moira, died last year of natural causes."

"She died of grief!"

"So you see, we know all about you, "Thomson said, closing the file and resting his clasped hands upon it.

"Ye don't know shit!"

The young man's venemous response boomed in the small interview room. In the bright striplighting the bruising round his eye looked dreadful and he nervously wiped a trail of bloody spittle from his chin.

"Why don't you tell me about tonight?" Thomson asked quietly. "Tell me what happened."

Farrell didn't reply.

"It might help you if you knew we've been watching you for a week, now; you, Tim Reilly, Peter O'Connor and James Gilvarry. Did you know Gilvarry's dead by the way? Very nasty. Big hole in the back of his head."

Farrell looked away.

"What was it, Ricky? A falling-out? Did you have a row and win the argument with a bullet?"

No response.

"I don't know, it seems an awful waste. Seventeen years old and now you'll be spending the rest of your life banged-up. Have you ever been inside a prison, Ricky? Can you imagine what it feels like when the cell door bangs shut and the light goes out and you're alone in the darkness? Think of the fear, waking up in a cold sweat and suddenly realising you're going to spend the rest of your days caged like an animal."

"Go t'hell."

"Of course, it won't be an Irish prison you'll be going to, you know that? You operated over here and here's where you'll serve. I must say I don't envy you, I don't envy you at all; you see they don't like terrorists, your common-or-garden villains. They class people like you in the same low bracket as rapists and child-molesters. Even lower. One day you'll be taking a shower, you'll be buggered and battered and no one'll come. You see, prison's full of deaf people, Ricky, and the warders are the deafest of them all.

"Having said that, if you were to co-operate we might make things a little easier. We'd see you safely locked away from those who'd want to do you harm, want to rip your eyes and balls out and garotte you like a dog. Make no mistake, son, that's exactly what would happen; and the tragic thing is no one'd care because nobody likes a terrorist."

"I won't talk!"

"Pity. And not very wise. Let me give you the lie of the land and see if I can't change your mind. You were found in a warehouse containing a shipment of automatic weapons and grenades; there was one man – a former British soldier – tied to a chair, and another man lying dead on the floor with a bullet in his skull. There was nobody else there, just you. You, a man who'd been forcibly abducted and a corpse. Sounds pretty damning, doesn't it?"

Farrell didn't reply, his eyes on the splintered desk before him, and Thomson rose and moved to the high barred window.

"Shall I tell you what a barrister will make of that in court? He'll say that you and James Gilvarry had arrived in England to kill and maim civilians. That you decided to get into practise by kidnapping a former member of Her Majesty's Armed Forces. That you and Gilvarry fell out, that you shot him dead in cold blood, that you pointed a pistol at his head and blew his life away. Of course, it was fortunate that the night-watchman heard the shot and called the police or you would no doubt have done to Mister Wilcox what you did to your erstwhile confederate Gilvarry. The police arrived and with admirable courage disarmed you and arrested you and thus saved the nation from your violence. The people in court will cheer and the papers will resurrect their campaign for the reintroduction of hanging."

"I didn't shoot Jimmy!"

"No one else was there."

"I was bloody well tied up, meself!"

"The police report won't mention any rope. And as for my people's role in this affair, well, we don't officially exist so all due credit for your capture will go to the police. Do you see what I'm driving at, Ricky? And then, of course, there's your sister."

Farrell, whose head was spinning, looked round at Thomson with alarm. "What d'ye mean?"

"Well, she's due to be reassessed in a few months' time and this will hardly help her case."

The fact that neither case was – or could be – connected didn't occur to Farrell. He was too wrapped up in confusion to think coherently; and through his fear and doubt he saw Maureen who had already served two-thirds of her sentence.

"Do you want to see her do the full stretch? It could happen, Ricky. One 'phone call and she'll do the bloody lot. An all because of you."

"No!"

"Think about it, son; think of Maureen rotting away, her flesh getting wrinkled and bruised with age. Do you want your sister to rot, Ricky? Do you want her to die a little every day?"

"No ..."

The boy was sobbing and Thomson, who had moved behind him, rested his hands upon his jerking shoulders.

"Then tell me what happened. Tell me what you know. We can start by going over what happened when you first arrived on the mainland ..."

Doctor Patel was shrugging into his overcoat when Patrick Kelly joined him by the front door. The hallway was littered with bags of plaster and the scent of paint hung heavy in the air.

"Thanks again, Doc. Much appreciated."

Patel wasn't happy. These were gunshot wounds. It was serious and it could mean trouble.

"This is the last time I come, Mister Kelly. Don't telephone me again. Do you understand?"

Kelly nodded and, removing a wad of twenty pound notes from his pocket, stripped off five and handed them across.

"Your friend is a lucky man," the doctor said. "That bullet could have destroyed his face."

"An' his shoulder?"

"Keep the wound clean like I showed you and it won't become infected. But he won't be able to use that arm again for some time. He must rest."

When he had gone Kelly returned to the back upstairs bedroom, the only serviceable one in the house. Reilly lay sedated on the cot, the left side of his face swollen and covered with a dressing and his right arm strapped to his side. Kelly studied him in silence, then nodded to Seamie who turned out the light and followed him out, closing the door quietly behind him. They would have to wait till the morning before they could find out what had happened, before they knew the extent of the damage to their cover and the danger they were in. Which meant that both would spend a sleepless night chasing ghosts through the halls of their fear, taking it in turns to watch over the unconscious Reilly.

It was midnight when Ricky Farrell finished talking. Thomson had taken copious notes and had watched without interest when the constable had entered to return the youth to his cell. He stretched and, packing up his briefcase, left the station and walked to the car which was waiting to ferry him home.

It had been one hell of a night, with one thing and another. First, Monica Tyndall providing the key to cracking the Perseus code; then the Provos snatching Wilcox minutes before Daniels and his Special Branch escort arrived to warn and protect him. At least the former SAS man was alive, which was more than could be said for Alan Pennick who was stretched out on a mortuary slab.

Farrell had said the snatch operation fell beyond their original remit and that Reilly had been furious when they had been ordered to carry it out. The arms shipment which Kelly had stored was to have been used to wreak destruction on both civil and military targets and he had believed that the folly of abduction would only have served to place their original function in jeopardy.

But as for the men who had arrived so fortuitously to rescue Wilcox, Farrell was ignorance itself. Which still left questions. Who were they and why had they appeared? Had Perseus sent them to protect his former linkman and by doing so protect his own identity? Or were they somehow connected with the arms? Thomson shook his head at the complexity of it all and thanked God that the larger stage had not been filled by an escalating game.

But there were still three terrorists missing, Reilly, Kelly and Seamus McGee. Peter O'Connor was recovering from his wounds in a prison hospital. Farrell had said that only Reilly, Gilvarry and himself had been present in the warehouse. The police had found a trail of blood leading to the window, which meant that Reilly had been hit in the firefight and where he had run to God only knew!

Although it was unlikely Kelly would return to his house in Gordon Road, Thomson had decided to keep it under observation as there was always the chance that he had not been alerted. Hospitals too were at this moment being visited by Special Branch officers looking for gunshot wounds. It wasn't likely they would find any — at least, not the ones they were seeking; but the procedure had to be followed, if only to ensure that all the bases were being covered.

Finally, a check had to be made into Kelly's crooked background. No doubt he had other properties registered under an alias or aliases.

Thomson believed that once they found out where they were, they would also find Reilly and McGee and wrap the whole thing up. But finding them would take time and not a little luck; though after tonight he was convinced that luck was with them. At least he hoped it bloody was.

But still there were questions. Who were the men who had rescued Peter Wilcox and why had they done it? And how did the IRA get hold of the information not only of the original operation, but also knowledge relating to the current whereabouts of the team which had been charged with running it?

Something was rotten in the State of Intelligence – someone had talked, had traded with the enemy. Lisburn would have to be notified, for only they kept operational records; but what they did not keep were records regarding the whereabouts of personnel once they had left the Service. Only Whitehall did that. Which meant that there were at least two leaks which needed to be traced and plugged.

Thirty minutes after leaving Paddington Green, Thomson was climbing into bed. It had been a long day and eventually he was graced with a sleep which put an end to the questions which harassed him.

Martin Kennedy was sitting alone in the dark in the front room of his cottage. It was raining again. It was always bloody raining. He listened to the swirling wind driving the water against the window, to the leaves on the trees in the garden rustling like a wild tambourine. There was a time when he might have enjoyed it, a time when he would have fallen asleep to the sounds of the weather lulling him into a state of deep relaxation. But all he could think of now was betrayal and the fact that one of the men whom he had trusted was a tout.

Suddenly, the back door opened and the wind howled through the cottage. Donal Brady entered pushing back the hood of his anorak.

"Mister Kennedy? Are ye there?"

"I want ye t'contact GHQ an' arrange a meetin'," the Chief said when Donal appeared in the doorway. "I also want a tail puttin' on every bloody man."

"Are ye sure that's wise? I mean, if word got out it could damage our standin'."

"Our standin's already shot t'hell! Now will ye do like I tell ye? I want t'know where they go an' who they talk to. I want 'em kept under constant surveillance an' I want 'em brought t'Daley's place one week from today."

Donal nodded. "I'll see that it's done." Then he went reluctantly back out into the rain.

When he had gone, Kennedy turned his head back to the window and listened to the car engine stutter into life and drive off into the distance. With all the shit that was flying at the Movement it was good to know that there was at least one person he could trust.

CHAPTER 20

PETER Wilcox woke at ten the following morning. His body felt like a sack of screaming bruises and his head rang like an impatient summons. Peeling himself from bed he winced as the pain hit – the slightest movement was harrowing and he screwed his eyes tight shut against it; then he went into the bathroom where he took a long cold shower, the jets of water needle-sharp, increasing his discomfort. But gradually the pain subsided and, twenty minutes later, he stepped from the cubicle and gingerly towelled himself dry.

Eleven o'clock and he was dressed and sitting in the front room watching TV. He didn't remember much of what had happened the previous night, but he recalled enough to recognise that the incident topping the news headlines was the one in which he had been involved. According to the report, a man had been found shot dead in a warehouse in Chiswick. Identified as one James Gilvarry, an active member of the Provisional IRA, police investigating the shooting believed it to be the result of a disagreement arising from an illegal arms deal. An arsenal of weapons and explosives had been impounded and they were holding a man for questioning.

The next item dealt with the recession and Wilcox pushed the standby. An illegal arms deal? Disagreement? He chuckled softly at the bullshit Five had fed to the press, then went into the kitchen where he poured another coffee.

Twenty minutes later, the doorbell rang. It was Jamie Daniels and two Special Branch detectives. Wilcox buzzed them in and returned to the front room where they found him sitting in the armchair by the window.

"How are you feeling this morning?" Daniels asked.

"How do you think I'm bloody feeling?" Wilcox replied sourly.

The young MI5 man who was genuinely concerned hovered uncertainly, then asked if they might sit down. Wilcox waved them to the couch and glared at them over his coffee cup.

"Look, I know you've been through hell," Daniels said, "but you were in no condition to give us a statement last night. Do you mind?"

Wilcox did – someone somewhere had cocked things up and he had brunted the consequences – but he gave one to them anyway.

Then he decided to ask some questions of his own which Daniels courteously answered, except, of course, for the reason behind the gunfight and his reprieve.

"And Farrell – that's the man we have in custody – doesn't know either."

"But you must have some idea?"

"It's possible Perseus wanted to protect himself, that he sent someone across to watch over you. We know you don't know who he is, but we don't think that he does."

"They didn't do a very good job of protecting Alan Pennick."

"Granted," Daniels replied. "But I only said that it was possible, not that it was definite. I mean, for all we know he might have sent someone over to kill you on the basis of a closed mouth catching no flies. One active service unit stumbling onto another, neither one knowing the other's purpose and they shoot it out. In all the violence you're forgotten. Maybe we'll never know what happened?"

Wilcox was uneasy. "If you're right about him wanting me dead, then there's every chance they'll try for me again."

"I don't think it's likely."

"I hope you're bloody right!"

"I'm sure of it. But if you want I can organise some protection?"

"No. Things are bad enough without a couple of coppers under my feet. No offence," he added to the SB men who shook their heads. "Like you say, it's unlikely they'll come after me again." And if they did he had his own men to protect him, men he trusted.

Daniels and his escort rose. "Right then, we'll get out of your hair. If you remember anything else you'll give me a call?"

Wilcox nodded. "By the way, how close are you to pulling Perseus out?"

"We haven't managed to contact him yet, but we're doing all that we can."

When they had gone, Wilcox thought about the man he had helped to run. The poor bastard was alone in the field with no one to talk to or support him. Although he wasn't really in danger – at least not from the men who had run him – he believed that his identity was going to be discovered and the fear alone would probably lead him into betraying himself.

Wilcox wondered what he would do if he were in the agent's shoes, denied contact with those who could rescue him, knowing he was being sought and what being found would mean. He tried to imagine the terror. The gnawing uncertainty, the sickening fear of knowing each new day could be his last. If he were Perseus and believed his former handlers could deliver him up to Provo vengeance and that an ASU had been despatched to ensure it, he would do what he damn well could to prevent it.

He shivered. Suddenly, he knew the agent hadn't sent someone to protect the men who had run him. Daniels was right: Perseus had sent someone to kill them, to buy a little time.

Operation Gorgon, its purpose to infiltrate the Provisional IRA; a strategem conceived a decade ago which had been too successful for now it had turned upon the men who had fashioned it.

And it wasn't over yet.

Emily Baker waited for the man from MI5. She had not been arrested; but that did not mean that she wouldn't be. She had spent all Sunday trying to convince herself that Patrick Kelly had nothing to do with the murder of Alan Pennick, that it was just a coincidence. But the more she had thought about it, the more she had been certain that, had she not supplied her lover with information regarding his domicile, the former Military Intelligence Officer would still be alive.

And that was more than her conscience was able to bear.

She had arrived at the office early as usual. Sam Deaves, the commissionaire, had greeted her warmly and asked her how she was keeping. She had smiled as she always did, masking the true state of her feelings; and then she had taken the lift to her Section on the fourth floor where, instead of going straight to her desk to pick up where she had left off on Friday, she had gone straight to her Supervisor, a kindly middle-aged man named Griffiths, and confessed.

It had been easier than she had expected. In a way it was a relief. Mister Griffiths had listened as she calmly told him what she had done; then he called Security who escorted her to an empty office beside the store room, an office where she waited for the man from MI5.

In spite of her fear, she was remarkably composed. As she stared at her cherry-red nails, her hands clasped loosely in her lap, she wondered what would happen to her, whether they would send her to prison or just fire her. Prison, probably, on a charge of treason. Was that what she had become — a traitress? She had done what she had because she was in love, not with another political system but a man who had used and deceived her. But she knew her motivation would seem unimportant when the act became known. She might not be a Philby or a Blunt, Burgess or Maclean, but that was where her name would belong. With other traitors.

At a little after ten o'clock, a short, middle-aged man with a kindly face stepped into the room, relieving the Security man with a nod. He sat down before her with a smile and took a pipe from his pocket.

"Good morning, Miss Baker," he said, "my name is Harry Thomson. I believe you have something you want to get off your chest ...?"

Patrick Kelly spent the day in a daze of apprehension. The radio had carried a report of an arms deal that had soured. One man dead and another in custody; that was all that was said. But Kelly knew the report for the bollocks it was.

What the bloody hell had happened? What the hell had gone wrong? A simple snatch had turned into a gunfight: one dead, one taken, and another shot to pieces lying unconscious up in the bedroom. Talk about a fuck-up! Finishing his second bottle of Bushmills, Kelly tossed the bottle into the rubbish in the front room corner. Jesus, he was so damn scared that he couldn't even get pissed!

At half-past four, Seamie came downstairs. "He's woken up, wants t'see ye."

"An I want t'bloody see him!"

Reilly, looking a hell of a state, was sitting up in the cot. Christ, thought Kelly, but his mother wouldn't recognise him. Staying in the doorway, he tipped a nervous nod.

"How's about ye, Tim?"

Reilly had difficulty speaking. The flesh had been torn from his cheekbone and the dressing on the wound was coloured a dirty shade of brown. He waved Kelly closer. God, but he looked bloody awful. The stench in the room was nauseating and it was all Kelly could do to keep from gagging.

"What time is it?" Reilly asked, his voice slurred as if he were drunk.

"Half-four."

"Ye have t'phone Donal. Tell'm it's all gone t'shit."

"What happened out there?" Kelly asked. "Was it the police who shot ye?"

Reilly shook his head. "Dunno who it was. He killed Jimmy, ye know?"

"I know. T'was on the radio."

"What're they sayin'?"

Kelly told him; and he also told him that the house in Gordon Road had been tumbled. Reilly stayed silent for a moment as he took it all in, considered it. Then he shut his eyes and drew a long, deep breath.

"Give Donal a call." He told him the procedure. "Tell'm the unit's busted wide. But we still have a chance t'nail the tout."

Kelly couldn't believe what he was hearing. "How?"

"Never mind. Jus' tell'm."

"Okay." Even in his weakened condition Reilly exuded authority. "I'll see it's done. Get some rest. I'll be up t'see ye later."

"How's he doin'?" Seamie asked when Kelly returned downstairs.

"He's a fuckin' madman, so he is! Jayzus, how the fuck did I ever get involved?"

A conduit, a pipline, a middleman, that's what Kelly was. He had never wanted to be a soldier, had never had the bottle. But now, thanks to Reilly, his security, cover, whole bloody life had been blown to fucking pieces. He was impaled on the sharp end and he had to find a way to wriggle off.

Donal had done what the Chief had asked. All twelve members of GHQ were under discreet surveillance. At the end of each shift the shadows were to report to a house off the Falls owned by the widow of a Provo martyr, an imprisoned man who had starved himself into the folklore of the Movement. Donal was to visit the house each night and then deliver his report to Kennedy in person. Billy McKee had been assigned to drive him there and back.

At six o'clock the telephone rang. The caller asked for Sean. Donal knew it wasn't Reilly, guessed that something had gone wrong and went to the 'phone-box on the corner to wait for the news. Some old biddy was shut up inside busily gabbing away and it was all he could do not to reach inside and drag her out into the rain.

After what seemed an eternity, she hung up and cheerfully stepped out.

"Ye'd think the angels'd get tired o'weepin' on the soil o'this poor country," she said. "If it doesn't stop soon, I'll be buyin' a boat, so I will. Are ye fair?"

"Aye, missus, I'm doin' fine. How's yourself?"

"T'was me son," she said. "Been livin' across the water an' he's comin' home. Sure, an' I don't know why he's botherin'. Who'd want t'come back t'this?"

She laughed and threw up the canopy of her umbrella and, bidding him farewell, hurried off down the street. Donal shook his head and wondered at the fortitude of the people of Belfast; then he stepped into the 'phone-box to wait for his call.

A few second later it came.

"Donal?"

"Who's that?"

"Pat Kelly. Tim couldn't make it."

Kelly explained what had happened ending with a string of oaths as he described his personal wreckage.

"What the fuck am I gonna do, Donal?" he whined. "I'm fucked t'death, so I am!"

"Are ye safe where ye are?"

"Safe?" I fuckin' hope so!"

"In that case stay put, d'ye hear? Do nothin'. Let me speak t'the Chief an' call me back tomorrow at the same time. Okay?"

"Okay."

Donal muttered reassurance, then hung up the receiver. Wilcox was alive, the ASU was burned; in six days' time a meeting would be held to smoke out the informer. Six days and it would all be over; but did he have six days?

It had to have been O'Malley who had whacked the ASU. The fact that Reilly and his team were out of commission was all to the good; but O'Malley had failed in the task he had been given. Now he would know that the men he had shot were members of the Movement on a mission. He would want to know why Donal had sent him when the Movement was interested in Wilcox. Far from killing the danger Donal had simply added to it by persuading O'Malley into acting for him. The web was spun and now he was in danger from a man who scared him more than any other.

He had to find a way out; it was all too bloody messy! He dug in his pockets for some change to call the contact number Tyndall had given him; but apart from his keys and a five pound note he hadn't got a penny on him.

Cursing, he backed out of the 'phone-box and ran back through the rain to get some coins from the jar in his kitchen. But when he turned the corner he found Billy McKee waiting to take him to the house in the Falls to collect the surveillance reports.

The call would have to be delayed and he shuddered as the fear cut through him. Time was running out and so was his luck.

It was almost half-eleven when Michael Finlay staggered home from the pub. Cutting through an alley on his way to Connaught Road, he stopped short when he saw a familiar figure standing before him.

"Jaysuzz, I thought they'd have ye by now!"

"Ye're a bloody fool, Michael," said O'Malley. "I wasn't goin' t'take her."

"Bullshit. Ye had your eyes on her since ye arrived."

"It's you she loves. Christ knows why, for ye're a lousy drunken bastard. But then, some women make a habit o'lovin' the wrong fellas."

O'Malley had stepped closer as he spoke until he was standing less than four feet away.

"Gonna shoot me?" Finlay asked, trying to hide his fear.

"I'm goin' t'do better than that," the smaller man replied. "I'm goin' t'let ye carry on the way ye are an' one day ye'll wake up an' she'll be gone. An' when that happens ye'll realise what ye've lost an' there'll be no one t'blame but yourself."

He had intended killing Finlay, but Onya had begged him not to. He had met her by arrangement that afternoon and she had tried to hide the bruises behind dark glasses and a headscarf. The damage had angered O'Malley, but she had defended her husband.

"He wasn't always like this," she had said. "He's disappointed, scared. You'll be gone an' he'll forget. Please don't make it difficult."

"It doesn't have t'be this way," he had told her.

"He needs me," she had whispered.

He had kissed her once goodbye and now he felt his anger burning brightly.

"Think of it, Michael," he said. "Every time ye take a drink ye're killin' her love. Every time ye treat her bad ye're losin' her."

Suddenly, his foot lashed out and drove into the big man's crotch. A cry of pain and he fell, doubled-up, into the dirt.

"But hear me well, Michael Finlay. If I ever hear ye've been slappin' her around, I'll come for ye. An' then it's more than a kick in the bollocks ye'll be gettin'."

Finlay rolled onto his back, his brawny hands cupped around his aching testicles; and when he finally opened his eyes, O'Malley had gone.

CHAPTER 21

ON Sunday evening, his condition having deteriorated, Jenny's father Tom had been admitted into hospital. Although doctor Markham their GP had tried to prepare both her and her mother for the inevitable, it had still come as a shock when, at two minutes past six the following morning, he had died.

The funeral was to take place at midday on Wednesday. It was to be a simple affair. Tom had never liked a lot of fuss. Just close family and a few good friends. Then a quiet drink to mark his passing. Things would never be the same. There would always be a vacuum.

Jenny had telephoned Peter who was driving down today. They were both concerned about David who had grown very close to his granddad. On learning of his death the boy had grown very pale. He wouldn't eat, he wouldn't talk; he seemed to have withdrawn into the void that death had left behind and nobody could reach him.

Wilcox arrived at ten o'clock and Jenny came to greet him. They embraced without speaking and he winced as she pressed against his ribs.

"What's the matter?" she asked. "Are you hurt?"

"It's nothing." He paused. "I'm sorry, Jen. Tom was a good man."

Inadequate, but what else could he say? Death took the polish off the glibbest tongue and he had never been eloquent.

Going inside, they found Marjory busy in the kitchen. She smiled when she saw him, but her eyes were sad. The sting of death did not hurt those it took, but those it left behind; for they were made to bear the loss, to carry on.

"Marjory, I'm so sorry."

"I miss him, Peter," she replied. "I don't know how I'll manage to live without him."

She started to cry and Jenny held her. Wilcox looked on helplessly. He felt like an intruder and withdrew.

As a soldier, he had witnessed death many times and sometimes he had even been its instrument. But this was different. It was family. This could not be shrugged off, disregarded.

He found himself remembering an incident in South Armagh. He had not been long commissioned and the patrol he had been leading had been fired upon. None of his men had been injured, but a young boy had been killed in the crossfire. The boy's mother had come running from the farmhouse and for as long as he would live he would remember the pain in her eyes and the keening sorrow which bled from her as the life flowed from her child. Although the inquiry had established that the fatal shot had not come from a soldier's weapon, the guilt of having been in part the cause of an innocent's death had stayed with him. As had the eyes of the mother. Marjory's had the same expression, a look of pained disbelief, of anger at the cruelty of her loss. Bitterness. Only death could fill an eye with such a desperate grief. To lose a loved one taught despair, bit deep into the psyche, and Marjory was a new girl in the classroom.

Through the sliding door in the living room, he saw David swinging listlessly on the tyre-swing suspended from a gnarled branch of the oak tree. Walking out, he crossed the lawn. The boy didn't see him approach.

"David?" No response. He reached out and turned the tyre towards him. "Hello, son."

From the kitchen, Jenny looked out anxiously. She watched him lift the boy from the tyre and cradle him like an infant. He looked so frail, vulnerable and small in his father's arms and it made her want to cry. But there would be time enough for tears. She had to be strong. For Marjory, she had to be strong.

The day passed as such days do, slowly, aimlessly, with effort. Come nightfall, when David was tucked up in bed, Wilcox joined Jenny out on the patio.

"Your mother thought you might like this," he said, placing a cardigan around her shoulders.

She hadn't noticed how cold it was. It was funny how such things went unregarded.

"David's asleep. He asked me to say goodnight for him."

"I wish he would cry," she said. "It's wrong to bottle it up."

"Give him time. Death's a difficult concept for a child to grasp."

"It's not exactly easy for adults."

For Jenny the hardest part to bear was the feeling that her father had deserted her. For as long as she could remember he had always been beside her, bandaging her knee when, as a child, she had fallen off her bicycle, right up to her divorce when it seemed that her life had come to an end. He had been a stabilising influence upon her, a presence she had relied upon, had trusted without question. She could not think of a single time that he had let her down and his loss, she knew, would only be truly felt in the years to come.

"It's a lovely night," she said. "Look at the moon."

Wilcox did. It was almost full and bright like yellowed silver, not a soldier's moon, but one for lovers, one for dreamers.

"Do you remember when Dad bought that telescope for David and he taught him the constellations? Do you remember how hard it was to get him off to bed because he wanted to look at the stars?"

"I remember," Wilcox replied, putting his arm around her. "And I also remember how we became as hooked as he was. What happened to it?"

"It was broken in one of the moves."

He remembered how he had always meant to replace it but had somehow never got around to it, like so many things he had meant to do he thought to himself with not a little bitterness.

A few moments passed in silence, then Jenny seemed to shake herself.

"We should get back inside. Mum'll get lonely by herself."

That night as Wilcox lay in bed, he heard the door open. A rustle of silk as she sloughed her robe and then she was lying beside him. They didn't make love. It wouldn't have been right. Instead, they held each other close, drawing comfort from each other. Wilcox felt his chest grow moist and knew that she was crying. He spoke a gentle word of comfort and then she let it go, all the emotion she had held in check, the grief, her slim body trembling with release.

The service took half-an-hour. When the cedar coffin had been lowered into the ground, the mourners traipsed off in a sombre line, pausing briefly before the family to murmur their condolences, towards the cars which were waiting to carry them away from this reminder of their own frail mortality.

Then came the funeral breakfast and they remembered a husband, father, father-in-law, grandfather and friend. It was an occasion to give thanks for a life and to mourn the passing of a presence which would always be remembered and never replaced.

And then it was over. Friends departed and, once again, the family was alone. Marjory went upstairs to rest. David went to his room and changed. Then he followed his parents into the woods as they took the dog for a walk.

It was a beautiful day. Sunlight sparkled on the surface of the river and the myriad scents of summer rode on the warm breeze. Wilcox and Jenny watched their son throw an idle stick for Brutus. He displayed none of his usual exuberance and it saddened them to see how death had touched his natural gaiety.

"How long can you stay?" Jenny asked.

Wilcox believed he could still be a target and did not want to endanger them.

"I have to go back tonight," he said.

She turned away and he saw that she was angry. He reached a hand towards her, then withdrew it knowing it would only be unwelcome.

"Look," he added. "I'll come back in a few days. We could all go away, you know, on a break to Wales or somewhere. What do you say?"

"David, keep away from the edge! I don't want you falling in, do you hear me?"

"Jen?"

"David! I won't tell you again!"

Reluctantly, the boy stepped back from the river and began to wander back along the path towards them. Brutus leapt up at him with the stick in his mouth, but David wasn't interested.

"Did you hear what I said?" Wilcox asked.

"I heard."

"And?"

"Fine. You do what you want to, Peter. You always have."

She turned and started back for home, David and Brutus close behind. Wilcox sighed and followed and, at six that evening, with nothing resolved, he clambered into his car and drove back to London.

CHAPTER 22

ON the day of Tom's funeral, the two young men followed Michael Donovan to a house in the suburbs of Belfast. It was his second visit in three days and Donal Brady had told them to stick to him like glue.

"Why?" Jimmy Rourke had asked. "What's he done?"

"Nothin' that concerns you," Donal had replied. "Jus' see ye don't lose him. Right?"

Andy Breen sat bored in the passenger seat. "Ye know what I think?"

"What?"

"I think he's givin' her one."

They had seen Donovan met at the door by a busty brunette with fuck-me eyes and legs like an overweight pony.

"Don't ye ever think of anythin' else?" Rourke asked.

"Sure an' what else is there t'think of, stuck in this bloody car?" He breathed a heavy sigh. "Wish it'd stop rainin'.

"I'm shit-tired o'listenin' t'your complainin'. Why can't ye jus' belt up an' read your book?"

"I finished it yesterday."

"So why'd ye bring it?"

"It's the only book I have."

Exasperated, Rourke leaned forward and turned the radio on. The car's interior was filled with Country and Western and, grimacing, he spun the dial to another station.

"Why'd ye do that? I like that music."

"It's my bloody car," Rourke replied. "We'll listen t'what I want t'listen to."

A moment later, he turned it off and sat back with a sigh.

"What's up?" Breen asked.

"Nothin'."

"Tell me."

"I said it was nothin', okay? Jus' mind your own business."

"Is it your Auntie Mary?"

"What?"

"Your Auntie Mary? Ye said she was taken t'hospital. Is she dead?"

"She bust her bloody ankle! Nobody dies from a busted ankle!"

Rourke looked like he wanted to thump him and Breen turned away with a shrug.

At ten-past five, they saw Donovan leave the house and run through the rain to his car. Rourke started his engine and they followed him to a bar in the City Centre.

"Every bloody time the same thing," Breen complained. "Work in the mornin', nookie in the afternoon, an' a skinful before dinner!"

They waited in the car until a quarter-to-six, then followed him home to the wife.

"Roll on six o'clock," said Andy Breen wistfully. "I'm starvin' an' me Ma's doin' lamb chops tonight ..."

Christy Keegan left his office at five and went home for his dinner. At half-past six he took a cab to the Sinn Fein advice centre in West Belfast where he listened to the usual complaints about leaking roofs, poor housing and delayed payments from the Social.

At nine o'clock, he left for a card game at a neighbour's place and then went home to his wife and bed. He didn't see the two men sitting in a van at the end of his street, nor did he realise he was being followed.

Eoin McCann was having a quiet drink in a waterfront bar when a couple of rowdies came in, half-cut and hungry for trouble. He watched them stagger to the bar from his seat in the corner. They were big boys in their early twenties with crewcuts and donkey jackets.

The barman eyed them nervously. "What'll it be, lads?"

"Gizza coupla pints," the dark-haired one said. "An' none o'that whore's piss ye keep in them bottles under the counter."

The barman filled two glasses from the pump and handed them across. "That'll be one-ninety."

The rowdy reached into his pocket and pulled out a handful of change. He selected a fifty-pence piece and four tens.

"There ye go," he said. "One ninety."

His blond companion laughed. It was a great crack! They downed their drinks and slammed the glasses back onto the bar.

"Same again."

The barman looked in mute appeal at his regulars, but they wouldn't meet his eye. So, with a nervous sigh, he replenished their glasses and moved across to the other end of the bar where he busied himself with a towel and a glass.

The dark man turned and surveyed the customers with a sneer.

"Regular bundle o'laughs, this crowd."

"Sure an' they don't look like they've moved off them seats in years," the blond replied.

"Hey, Grandad!" said the dark one to an old bearded man at a table by the door. "Don't ye find it hot with all them pubes on your face?"

Jesus, but he was on form tonight. He was shit-bloody hot!

"Maybe he likes lookin' like a wanker?"

"Better duck if he strokes his throat," the dark one replied and they howled and brayed with laughter. Then they turned back to the bar and finished their drinks. "Hey, barman! Giz another round!"

The barman shook his head. "Sorry, lads, but I think ye've had enough."

"D'ye hear that, Timmy?" the blond said, his voice laced with menace. "This Taigh bastard says we're pissed!"

The one called Timmy leaned across and took the barman by the scruff of his neck.

"Pissed is it?"

"C'mon lads. I don't want no trouble."

"I don't want no trouble," Timmy mimicked.

Suddenly, he hauled the small man over the bar and dumped him on the floor.

"Hey, Pat, look at your man grovellin' down there. I think maybe he wants t'clean some o'this Catholic shite off your boots."

Pat lifted his soiled boot and pressed it against the barman's face.

"Lick it," he said; and when the barman turned his face away: "I said fuckin' lick it, d'ye hear?"

They didn't see McCann rise from his seat and walk up behind them.

"Why don't you boys jus' go on home?" he said. "Ye've had your fun. Leave it at that."

"D'ye hear that, Timmy?" He's tellin' us t'leave."

Timmy stepped over the prostrate barman and stuck out his whiskery jaw.

"Maybe he'd like t'make us?" he said.

Suddenly, McCann's fist shot out and smashed into his face, followed quickly by a stamping kick to his knee. There was a vicious cracking sound as the patella was displaced and Timmy collapsed with a cry, knocking Pat against the bar.

"Jayzus!" he cried. "It was only a joke! Jus' a laugh!"

Timmy's mouth and nose were smeared with blood and Pat helped him struggle to his feet.

"Let's get out o'here," he sobbed; and when Pat didn't move: "C'mon!"

When the door had crashed shut behind them, McCann stooped down and raised the shaken barman.

"Y'okay, Mickey?" he asked.

"I'm fine," the barman replied, rubbing his neck. "But I think I'm in the wrong bloody business!"

When McCann walked home he didn't see the man on his tail. Wee Jimmy had watched the whole thing through the window and was determined to stick to the shadows.

Patrick Wheelan had had a row with his wife and had gone to spend the night with his girlfriend. Her name was Brenda and she was the horniest little bitch in God's creation. Her old man worked the night-shift as a security guard for a building contractor and Wheelan made the most of his absence.

"Come here," he said

"I will not, ye dirty beast. It's almost one an' I have t'get up for work in the mornin'."

They had already screwed three times that night, but Wheelan was greedy for more. Reaching across the bed, he tried to draw her towards him.

"Get off! I told ye I'm up in the mornin'!"

She had the biggest udders this side of a cow and he kissed them hungrily. She laughed, gave him a playful swipe and he rolled on top of her.

"Brenda O'Hare, I love ye!"

"I know what you love, ye filthy wee bugger!"

Suddenly, he disappeared beneath the blankets. Screaming with laughter, she brought her knees up cracking the underside of his jaw.

"Ouch! What the hell d'ye do that for?"

"Ah, is poor baby's chinny sore? Here, let Mommy rub it better."

Wheelan scowled and pushed her away. Then he reached over to the bedside table and lit a cigarette.

"Christ, I told ye not t'smoke in here," she complained. "Danny packed it in last week an' he's sure t'smell it."

"Sod Danny," he replied, two streams of smoke curling sullenly from his nostrils.

He left at six and drove back home. He knew Maeve would be waiting for him at the top of the stairs the second he keyed himself in, with the babby in her arms, curlers in her hair and the venom in her voice.

Cursing, he pulled the doorkey from his pocket and let himself in. He hadn't noticed the blue Mini rolling to a halt behind him.

Dermot O'Shea spent a quiet night in. Mary had taken the kids to her mother's for the week and he was sitting in his front room with the curtains drawn, his slippered feet upon the walnut coffee table, a drink in his hand and Bruch's Violin Concerto on the stereo.

There were two men sitting in a battered grey van outside. They had followed O'Shea to the station in the morning when he had put his family on the train to Donegal and then they had tailed him to work.

They had been surprised when they had been ordered to keep tabs on O'Shea, but had been smart enough not to ask why. They sat in silence sipping hot coffee from a thermos while they waited for the relief team to arrive.

It was midnight when Kennedy crawled into bed. Donal had driven over earlier that evening with the latest surveillance reports; but apart from the usual boozing and adultery, there had been nothing untoward.

It had been a long day and he turned off the bedside light. The branches of the tree outside his bedroom window tapped like skeletal fingers on the window pane and he lay awake with his hands tucked behind his head, unable to think of anything but revenge on the man the Brits had codenamed Perseus.

All it took was one mistake, one little slip-up and they had him. No one was perfect and a tout could not afford to be careless; but touts were afraid, they were scared wee shites and their fear always betrayed them in the end.

And Perseus was scared. Kennedy was sure of that. He knew how living a lie could wear you down, how the isolation finally put cracks in the veneer. And when that happened there was no re-firing the glaze; they just got wider and deeper until they were yawning gaps which could no longer be hidden and that was when they tripped.

In four days' time there was a meeting of GHQ. With luck they would have found him before then. If not, then there would be a bloody witch hunt; and no one would be leaving till he was found.

CHAPTER 23

FRANK Davis had spent the night on the cot in the corner of his office. He hadn't intended sleeping there, but he had been busy shuffling papers till nearly two a.m.; and what with the damn rain chucking it down by the bathful and the fact that he had mislaid his umbrella, he had reluctantly settled for the cot.

Of course, he felt like shit. He always did when he passed a night in the office. The cot was an army cast-off which needed re-springing and he wasn't getting any younger. A few years ago, when he had been young and horribly keen, a cot was just another exciting part of the Intelligence experience. But seasoning had put an end to all of that; especially when he had learned how boring life as an IO could be. Which is why he was usually at pains to make things as comfortable as possible. He cursed and swung his feet to the floor.

As any toil-junkie will tell you it is wise to keep a washbag in the desk. It is also wise to keep an electric razor, a clean shirt and a change of socks. When he had availed himself of all of these, Davis at least looked a little better. But he still felt like shit. Three cigarettes and an alka-seltzer later he began to feel human. Then he considered finishing what was left of the sandwiches he had bought yesterday tea-time. They were chicken salad and mayonnaise. A suspicious sniff and a look at the limp dry strings of lettuce was enough to dissuade him and he fed them to the bin. A fry-up would be much more gratifying.

Thus decided, he went to the desk where he collected his wrinkled grey jacket off the back of the chair and was halfway to the door when the 'phone rang. For a moment he considered leaving it, but his conscience wouldn't allow him to; so, going back and perching on the corner of the desk, he snatched up the receiver.

"Yes?"

Donal Brady's nerves were badly frayed. For the past few days he had barely had a moment to himself. Kennedy had him running about like a turkey ducking the axe, visiting the Shadows and collecting surveillance reports, and all the while he was being dogged by Billy McKee.

He hadn't been near a 'phone since Monday night. He hadn't even been home. Moira would be doing her nut and he would cop it good when he saw her. But that was the least of his problems. He knew that time was running out, that he was operating outside the safety-margin and had been for some time. He had to make contact with whoever it was who was running him and he had to do it fast.

They passed a call-box. It was risky, but he had no choice.

"Pull over," he ordered.

"What?" McKee was minding the bloody idiot driving in front of them.

"I said pull over."

The young man braked and swung into the gutter. "What for?"

"I have t'make a call."

"Who to?" He was suspicious.

"The wife, not that it's any o'your business. She'll be climbin' the bloody wall."

"Well, be quick about it. I can't stop here."

"Five minutes," Donal said; then he jogged back down the road to the 'phone.

"Yes?" The voice was unfriendly, tired.

"Gimme the man in charge," Donal said. "An' hurry, will ye? I haven't much time."

"Who is it?"

"Tell'm Perseus. Ye get that? Perseus!"

With all thoughts of breakfast driven from his head, Frank Davis moved around the desk to the chair.

"Do you know how long we've been trying to get hold of you?"

"Never mind that, now. Are you the man?"

"Yes."

"Good. Now listen. Ye've got t'get me out. Fast. D'ye hear? They're bloody well after me. They've got the dogs out an' they know bloody everythin'!"

"Okay," Davis said, reaching for a pen. "Tell me where we can meet you."

"Ye can't. That's just it. I'm being' dogged. I can't slip away."

"Well, what do you want us to do? Organise a lift?"

A common enough practice.

"No. I'm movin' all the time. Look, d'ye have a pen?"

"Yes."

"Right, well take this down. There's goin' t'be a meetin'. Sunday night. GHQ. All the big bastards, ye know?"

"What's it about?"

"Chief thinks one o'them's the tout."

"Which means your cover's still intact, yes?"

"Aye, but not for long. They've got the dogs out an' it's only a matter o'time before they get me. Christ, the way I'm feelin' I'll probably give meself away!"

"Well don't do that for God's sake," Davis said, busy scribbling away. "We'll have you safely out before you know it. Now, where's this meeting taking place?" Donal told him.

"And this farm's owned by a man called Daley?"

"Joe Daley, He's on your books. Did a stretch for possession back in the eighties."

"And the time of the meeting?"

"I'm not sure, but I think it's in the evenin'."

"Right. And you'll be safe till then?"

"I bloody hope so!"

Davis could hear the fear in his voice. He was obviously close to breaking. Would he be able to hold out?

"Look," he said, "I need your name. If we – "

"My name?" Donal was incredulous. "Ye've already got my bloody name!" McKee was leaning on the horn and he turned and waved impatiently. "I have t'go. Don't forget. Seven o'clock, Daley's place. Okay?"

Before Davis could reply, the informer hung up and was running back to the car.

"Took your time," McKee said.

"Shut your bloody gob an' drive," Donal said, fastening his seatbelt. They pulled out into the traffic and, as they drove away, Frank Davis was wondering how they could safely rescue a man whose identity they didn't know when the bullets would be flying indiscriminately.

Patrick Kelly shook his head.

"Ye're bloody mad!" he said.

Tim Reilly, out of bed and, pale as death, was leaning on the wall.

"Where are my trousers?" he said.

"The doc said ye needed rest. Don't go pushin' it till ye're ready."

"I am ready. Now, tell me where my trousers are, or so help me God I'll take the ones ye're standin' up in."

Kelly looked down and saw he was holding a gun.

"Jesus Christ, they're in the cupboard," he said, fear washing through him like a laxative. "An' go easy with that thing, will ye, or these trousers won't be fit for wearin'!"

Getting David to school was hard at the best of times, but since the death of his granddad it was murder. Screaming defiance, she had forced him into his uniform and was now getting ready to collect him. The Headmaster had told her she could keep him off till Monday – that under the circumstances it might be better if she did – but Jenny felt she had enough to cope with as it was and so she had made him go to school.

Marjory was resting in the spare bedroom. Since the funeral she had not stepped into the room in which she and Tom had slept, except to fetch a few things, clothes and the like, as there were too many things there to remind her of what she had lost. Jenny knocked.

"Mum?"

There was no response and she turned the handle. The curtains were drawn against the sun and Marjory was lying full-clothed on the bed.

"I'm just going to pick David up. I won't be long."

Again her mother didn't respond and approaching Jenny saw that she was crying.

"Oh, Mum ..."

To live with someone all your life, to share things and rely upon each other, and then to have that person disappear, to be forced to carry on alone, was a terrible thing. Would it be better, she wondered, if people were incapable of forming such close attachments? At least then death would seem less cruel, its effects would be a lesser burden to hold. God, but it was all so unfair.

When she had been married to Peter she had known that he would always be at risk. Especially when he had joined the SAS. She had lain awake at nights, wondering where he was, what he was doing, whether he was in danger, why the hell he had volunteered. Married men had no right going off playing dangerous games; especially when there were children to consider.

Children ...

They had had a daughter once: Victoria Jane who had died in the cot aged thirteen months. Jenny had been forced to cope alone as he was gadding about in some remote trouble-spot; she had never quite been able to forgive him for that. Then, two years later, his C.O., Colonel Flowers, had paid a night-call. Peter had been seriously wounded in a firefight in Northern Ireland and suddenly she had known she could not take it any more. Her worst nightmare — Peter's death — had almost become a reality. Many had thought her heartless when she asked him for a divorce, but for Jenny there was just no other course.

But losing someone you loved through a divorce was different from losing them in death. At least Peter had survived, was still around; but Tom was dead and Marjory was alone. Well, not quite alone — she had Jenny and David — but the fact remained she had lost the man she loved. Now she would have to find the strength to cope, to carry on, to mourn her love and to learn to look beyond it.

She sat for a while trying to comfort her mother, then gave her a kiss.

"I won't be long."

Then she went downstairs and took the car keys from the peg inside the hallway and a minute later was driving up the road.

David was sitting alone on the steps to the main school building. The day's end bell had sounded twenty minutes ago and his friends had already gone home. She waved, but he didn't wave back, merely stood, picking up his satchel, while he waited for her to turn the car around.

"Hello, love," she said as he strapped himself into the seat. "Sorry I'm late. did you have a good day?"

He shook his head and, seeing his disinclination to talk, she put the car into gear and drove away.

Five minutes later as they were winding through Frensham Lane she saw a white Cortina stopped at the side of the road. A man appeared from behind its sprung bonnet, waving her down; and, braking, she pulled in behind it.

"What's up?" she asked, winding down the window.

"Engine died on me," the man replied with a sheepish grin. "Would ye happen t'know if there's a garage hereabout?"

"There's one about a mile away. If you like I— "

Suddenly, the passenger door opened and a man with a dressing on his face and right coat sleeve hanging loose appeared with a gun in his hand.

"Get out o'the car, Mrs. Wilcox," he lisped. "Don't make a fuss an' ye won't get hurt."

David screamed and Jenny, pulling him across to her protectively, cried, "Who are you? What do you want?"

Patrick Kelly opened her door.

"Quickly, now," he urged. "Before he loses his temper."

Shocked into silence, she obeyed and they were dragged to the Cortina where another man, a young man, had appeared behind the wheel. They were thrown into the back. Kelly dropped the bonnet and jumped into the front passenger seat. Reilly climbed in beside them, his gun pressed into Jenny's side, and then they were speeding away, her car abandoned with its engine running.

CHAPTER 24

IT was Jacko who answered the 'phone. He and Mike Travis, the huge ex-Para, had been with Wilcox most of the day, listening to what had befallen him and discussing what precautions could be taken to keep him out of further danger.

"'Ullo?"

"Peter?"

"No, luv; Jacko. Jenny, innit?" He cupped his hand over the mouthpiece. "It's Jenny."

Wilcox rose and took the 'phone. "Jen? Is everything—"

"Wilcox?" A man's voice.

"Who's that?"

"Listen carefully. We have your wife an' son. If ye want t'see 'em alive again, ye'll tell us who Perseus is."

"Bastards have taken her and the boy," he said to Jacko and Mike. Then: "I've already told you. I don't know who he is!"

"Peter ...!"

Jenny's voice was followed by a scream. Wilcox felt the fear rise up within him and an anger he was unable to keep from his voice.

"Listen you bastard, if you hurt them you're bloody well dead! Do you hear me?"

"Twelve hours, Wilcox," the man said. "Ye've twelve hours t'decide what's more important: the tout or your family."

Suddenly, the line went dead.

"Hello ...? Hello ...!"

He slammed the receiver down and turned to face Jacko and Mike. He didn't speak – couldn't find the words; and Jacko, seeing his despair, rose and placed a bony hand on his shoulder.

"Don't you worry, Boss," he said. "We'll get 'em back. Won't we, Mike?"

Travis nodded darkly. "And then we'll kill the bastards!"

Patrick Kelly shook his head and turned away from the 'phone. He didn't like what Reilly had done; he didn't like it at all. He watched as Seamie pushed the woman and her kid towards the stairs; the boy was crying, holding fast to his mother's hand, and Seamie, the damn wee shite, was obviously revelling in the terror their abduction was causing them.

Christ, he had tried talking Reilly out of it! But Reilly had been in no mood for a discussion. The bastard was half-crazed with pain from the wounds he had received in the warehouse; a lunatic light seemed to blaze in his eyes and the only reason Kelly had agreed to go along with it all was because he was scared bloody shitless.

When he had learned what Reilly was planning he had tried to telephone Donal. On Tuesday night he had used the code, but a woman had answered, probably Moira. No, no one called Sean lived there. He had waited five minutes. Then he had called the 'phone- box. It had rung and no one had picked the 'phone up and, cursing, he had tried again the following night. The same thing had happened. Moira answered. He had asked her could he speak to Sean. Then, when she was about to hang up, he had thrown all caution aside and had asked if he might have a word with Donal. On identifying himself she had told him that the bugger hadn't been home for three days and, not knowing where he was calling from, said that if he saw him he was to tell the lousy stop-out that his bloody dinner was burnt and that had been that.

He had considered lying to Reilly, telling him Donal wanted it called off. But what if Reilly had checked himself? What if Donal had thought the snatch a good idea? The probable repercussions of such a deceit had persuaded him into obedience. Things were bad enough for him without him making them worse. But all the same, as he watched the captives climbing the stairs and Reilly glowering at them from below, he felt a terrible sense of foreboding.

Harry Thomson, sitting in the easy-chair in his office, looked contented. An arms shipment confiscated, a Provo ASU, destroyed, one of the leaks in the Intelligence question plugged and the man who had been the cause of it all had finally decided to make contact. All in all, not a bad result; although there were still some missing pieces.

God, but it had been a near-run thing. If Six had lost the shipment they would never have known about the ASU. A cynical thought, but it was fortunate that the IRA had stumbled onto Perseus since it had led to the bloody dismantlement of a cell whose primary purpose was to wage war on the mainland. Who did they have to thank for that? he wondered, lighting his pipe. Whoever it was deserved a bloody medal.

His thoughts then turned to the foolish Emily Baker. It had been decided not to place her under arrest, nor would she be trundled off to gaol. Her punishment lay in the unemployment line and in knowing she had unwittingly aided in the death of Alan Pennick. No doubt there were some who thought she had been let off lightly; but Thomson knew better – he had seen her remorse. He knew she would never be able to forgive herself for what had happened, for having misplaced not only her love but also her working integrity.

Peter Wilcox, now there was a man with the devil's own luck! Abducted and battered, then pulled from the maw of death by a person or persons unknown. Jamie Daniels had confided his fears regarding the former SAS man's safety and Thomson had agreed to short-term monitoring. But he doubted if it necessary.

Missing pieces ...

Where the hell had Reilly, Kelly and McGee disappeared to? They still had the O.P. running in Gordon Road, but it was highly unlikely Kelly would return. Thomson had men sifting through his tax-returns and banking records, and Special Branch were interviewing known associates. But nothing had turned up. Yet. It would only be a matter of time. He knew that. No one moved through life without leaving a trail of footprints behind them, however well disguised, and if Special Branch looked hard enough they would get him.

Earlier that day, another report had crossed his desk regarding the presence at an address in West Ealing of a terrorist suspect named Sean O'Malley. Thomson had paid it but cursory heed, merely pausing to wonder what had prompted the singular bluster of activity among the Irish Players. There had been no further developments and until there were it was pointless wasting mental energy on it. He had handed it, along with the Gorgon data, to Jamie Daniels who had filed it all away.

An arms shipment confiscated, a Provo ASU destroyed, and one of the leaks in the Intelligence dam well and truly thumbed.

Yes, he reflected, it had been a good result; and then he turned his thoughts to the Cabinet Minister's libidinous indiscretions.

The boat was waiting in the harbour ready to ferry O'Mally to the Cornish trawler lying at anchor half-a-mile from the shore.

"Are ye sure ye won't come?" he asked.

Cleary shook his head. "I'll fight for Ireland, but there's bugger all there for me. 'Sides, I've a cousin up north who's been after me t'visit. Then I fancy Scotland. They hate the English almost as much as we do."

O'Malley laughed as they shook hands.

"Take care o'yourself," he said. "An' if ye hear the hounds, run safely."

"So long."

Cleary watched him clamber into the boat and listened as it chugged away into the darkness. Then, stuffing his hands deep into the pockets of his reefer coat, he turned and wandered back to the place where he had parked.

Thirty minutes later the trawler got underway, its robust body battered by the swell. From a rail beside the wheelhouse, O'Malley watched the lights on the Cornish coastline; they looked like strings of coloured pearls on a jeweller's black felt mounting. By dawn he should be back in Ireland. The thought made him smile grimly, for his nostalgia for the place of his birth was overshadowed by the knowledge of what he must do. Donal Brady had sent him to the mainland to kill a man because of what he knew; and although O'Malley did not know precisely what that knowledge was, he had a name, Perseus, and guessed that Donal was that man, that Donal had been playing a game on both sides of the net, and now the time had come to settle the account.

It wasn't easy but they managed it, the mini arsenal spread out on the table in the kitchen.

"Some of it borrowed, some of it bought," said Jacko, while Wilcox looked it over.

There were two nine-millimetre high-power Browning automatics, a Colt .38 and a Second World War Luger, a real collector's item. But the pride of the collection was a Springfield rifle with a re-modelled stock and a telescopic sight.

"Dizzy can use the Springer," Jacko said. "'e might've been a sailor but 'e shoots like Annie Oakley. Got the bleedin' 'air for it any'ow. Ain'tcha, Diz?"

"Piss off," Greaves replied, tying his hair back into a ponytail.

"Now, since it's you who'll be meetin' 'em," the ugly cockney said to Wilcox, "you'll be needin' somethin' small you can 'ide an' draw quick if you need to. So, if you take the Colt, me an' Mike'll 'ave the Brownin's, which means the Luger's all yours, Charlie, right?"

Kane nodded. "I always wanted one o'these." He picked it up and smiled as he examined it, his gingery features softening with pleasure.

It was two a.m. The call was due at eight. Wilcox finished his whisky and dropped the tumbler into the plastic bowl in the sink.

"Best try and get some sleep," he said. He knew he wouldn't manage to, but rest was something he needed to have to weather the coming ordeal. "I'll see you in the morning."

They bade him goodnight and he retired to his bedroom where he sat on the bed, his mind awhirl with apprehension. Something told him he should have contacted the authorities, told Jamie Daniels what was going down. But instinct told him otherwise. The authorities had made a right pig's ear of everything to do with this bloody mess so far, and he wasn't going to take the risk of them cocking this up, not where his family was concerned. No, far better that he handled this himself. He was a trained soldier with a soldier's pride, as were his men; they were the cream, special forces, the elite — and if they couldn't handle it then no one bloody could. It was that simple. Jenny had been scathing about his calling, his vocation; but it was precisely this that would save her life and the life of their son. Fear of failure niggled away at the back of his mind, but he pushed it away. He couldn't afford to entertain it, not when so much was at stake. He closed his eyes and tried to empty his mind.

At eight o'clock, the telephone rang. Wilcox sprang from the bed and, running to the sitting room, snatched up the receiver.

"Wilcox?"

"You win. I'll give him to you, but not on the 'phone."

There was a long pause. He heard voices, muffled, indistinct, and then the man came back.

"Where?" he asked.

Wilcox relaxed. They were in with a chance.

"An abandoned airfield outside Bedford. Place called Apstead. Bring Jenny and David, then we can deal."

"Ye're in no position t'make deals."

"But I am in a position to show good faith," Wilcox replied. Here was his trump card and he prayed to God that it would work. If it didn't ... "Five are on to you. You've been under observation for a couple of weeks. One of your people talked. They know all about you. They know you killed Pennick."

Jamie Daniels would have cartwheeled in despair had he known how Peter Wilcox was using the information he had given him. There was another pause; then:

"Two hours. But mind ye come alone. Any funny business an' your wife an' son are dead."

Disconnected, Wilcox cradled the receiver. The time for action had begun and, feeling his chest tighten uncomfortably, he led the way out to the cars.

CHAPTER 25

THE aerodrome at Apstead was a relic of the past. A hundred-and-fifty acres of wilderness, its pitted runways were weathered and uneven with weeds pushing out through the cracks. The windows of the control tower and surrounding buildings were broken and the long corrugated hangars were brown and holed with rust and ready to collapse.

Apstead had been abandoned in 1953. Too small to hold a fully-operational jet-fighter squadron, the RAF had decided it wasn't cost effective and, in the sixties, a local flying club had taken it over; but they had been forced to move elsewhere when the site had been sold to developers.

Wilcox drove through the broken perimeter gate and parked before the control tower, cutting the engine and watching as the long grass rippled in combed waves in the breeze. It was a desolate place. In 1941-5, warplanes had rolled off the production lines to be delivered here for ferrying to squadrons based around the English countryside. This ground had shivered beneath the powerful engines of Blenheims and Lancasters. Spitfires and Hurricanes as they taxied down the runways to begin their operational lives. Now the field was silent, its original purpose but a memory which rotted, like its hangars and barracks, worn and outdated and soon to be forgotten like the people who had worked there.

"Boss ...?"

Jacko and the others had already left the car and were awaiting instructions regarding their deployment. Wilcox clambered out and ran a practised eye over the ground.

"Dizzy, take the tower. Mike, you and Charlie take those hangars to the right, and Jacko, you can take yourself off to that hut."

The men dispersed, all but Tyler who hovered uncertainly.

"You okay, Peter?" he asked. It was rare for him to use Wilcox's Christian name; he usually called him 'Boss', the informal term of address used by SAS enlisted men to their officers.

"I'm fine; it's Jenny and David I'm worried about."

"Well, don't be. We've got the ground well covered. Jus' make sure you keep 'em on this patch."

A nod, then the cockney was jogging away to his position. Wilcox checked his watch. It had just gone half-past nine. His nerves would not allow him to stand still and he walked across the cracked flags into one of the hangars.

It was a cavernous shed with a high round roof and, but for the tangle of weeds which had grown up through the floor, it was empty. His footsteps echoed in the silence and when he reached the centre he turned and stared about him. Once there had been rows of benches stacked with pots of grease and engine parts, ground crews standing on sturdy wings as they wielded spanners and the sounds of engines coughing into life, spinning propellers washing the dusty air. But now there was nothing but the birds who nested in the rafters. He wandered back out and made his way to the control tower.

The door was broken and held in place at the bottom by a single rusty hinge. He pushed it open and found himself standing in a short corridor, painted white and peeling with age, which led to a concrete railed staircase. Walking towards it, he passed by three rooms which had once been offices. Only one room still had a door and it was painted a dull green.

The tower itself was a square-shaped room whose windows gave a full view of the airfield. The ceiling was low with the flex of a single socket supporting a battered tin shade and no bulb; and on a stool in the corner sat Dizzy Greaves, feeding the clip of his rifle.

"A poor place, but home," he said as Wilcox stepped inside. He was a strange character, Dizzy — public school, from a landed family in Kent — he should have been an officer, but he had preferred the anonymity of the ranks, much to his father's disapproval who had been Colonel of a regiment in the Guards. *And* he had joined the Marines.

Wilcox had never managed to find out the truth behind his nickname. Mike said he had once tried out for the Paras but had succumbed to vertigo while training on the frame; Jacko reckoned the former Marine had caught a dose on leave in Singapore, the disease — or 'diz' — providing the handle he was known by. Not very likely, but considerably less prosaic. Dizzy had only been with the team for three-and-a-half months and Wilcox, who suddenly realised how little he knew the man, was about to satisfy his curiosity when he heard the sound of a car approaching. Looking out, he saw a white Cortina and his heart gave a sickening lurch as the reality of why they were there pressed home.

"Showtime," Dizzy said, ramming the magazine home and working the bolt.

Wilcox nodded. "Don't forget. If you get a clear shot, then take it. Otherwise, stay the hell away."

"Shit!"

"What?"

"The bastard's parked behind the hangar. If I'm to have any kind of a shot, you'll have to draw them out into the open."

His mouth dry and his belly tight, Wilcox left the tower checking the load of his sub-nosed .38. The sun was bright as he stepped out into the killing ground. Suddenly, the enormity of what he had undertaken reached out to him and he fought to control his fear. He and the boys were the only thing which stood between Jenny's and David's deaths and, hiding his weapon in the waistband of his trousers, he walked out into the open.

"That's far enough!"

The sun was in his eyes and he raised a hand to shade them.

"Where's my wife and son?"

Through the glare he saw a group of figures standing by the hangar. He began to walk towards them, but again the voice barked out.

"I said that's far enough!"

"Okay, take it easy. Just show me that they're all right."

A moment passed, then they started to move. From the control tower, Dizzy dropped his thumb to the safety-catch and peered through the scope. "Come on, you bastards," he muttered, "come on," willing their feet to carry them into the kill-zone. One clear shot was all he needed and their fear would take care of the rest.

Meanwhile, Mike and Charlie worked their way around the back of the hangars. Jacko was the first to see them. Resting his double- handed grip against the side of the hut, he trained his pistol on Patrick Kelly and waited for Dizzy to start it. But then the group stopped moving. They were only a couple of yards from the open ground and Jacko, feeling the sweat break out on his forehead, swore softly.

"Peter ...?" Jenny called, her voice trembling with fear.

"Jen? Are you okay? Is David?"

"Yes"

"The name!" said Reilly.

"First you have to let them go!"

Reilly grabbed hold of a handful of Jenny's hair and, clapping his pistol to the side of her head, stepped out into the open.

"Don't say I didn't warn ye!"

Suddenly, three cars turned into the airfield and sped towards them. The rest happened quickly, all precautionary measures cast aside. Dizzy fired, but the bullet missed as Reilly jerked into action. Jenny pushed free and ran to David and Jacko sprinted from cover, shouting.

"Jenny, get down!"

Reilly aimed his gun at the cockney, his finger jerking back on the trigger. But as he fired, Patrick Kelly stumbled into him and the shot went wide. Another shot. Kelly fell dead at his feet, a messy hole where his left eye had been, and in the tower Dizzy Greaves smoothly reloaded his rifle.

In the meantime, Peter Wilcox had begun to run towards them, pulling the Colt from his waistband and the hammer back to fire. Reilly banged off two wild shots, missed, then ran safely up the path between the hangars, Mike and Charlie missing him by a second.

But they caught Seamie. He was unarmed and, shaking violently, threw his arms up in surrender. Mike, the momentum of his run adding to his enormous physical power, swung his foot into the terrorist's crotch and Seamie folded into the air and was unconscious before he hit the ground. Continuing his run, he swerved and trained his gun on Kelly, while Charlie, carrying straight, came to a halt astride Seamie, his arms extended and his Luger pistol ready to fire a shot into his head.

Jenny and David lay in the shadow of the hangar. The boy was whimpering and Jenny was shielding him from danger with her body lying across him.

Wilcox knelt beside them, placed a hand upon her back. She screamed and fought as he tried to turn her over.

"Jen, it's me!"

Jacko, meanwhile, had taken off after Reilly. They had left the hangars behind and were moving through the old barracks complex. He had lost sight of the terrorist and, with pistol held in readiness, cautiously picked his way through the debris on the path lest he give his presence away.

The first building was clear. Looking carefully in through the shattered windows as he passed, he saw no sign of the terrorist. He crossed to the second, heart thumping, breathing laboured, but again there was nothing; and, the sweat now pouring from his face, he made his way silently to the third.

Reilly was tormented by pain. The wound in his face had opened up and he tore away the dressing sending a spray of blood onto the path. His right shoulder was aching where he had cannoned off one of the hangars and the lunatic light in his eyes which Kelly had seen and been afraid of seemed to grow in intensity as the agony coursed through his body.

A tract of woodland bordered the airfield and he knew that if he could make it through the buildings and across the fifty yards of open field he would be safe. Stepping from cover, he saw Jacko crossing the path directly opposite him and clumsily raised his weapon. He couldn't miss.

Wilcox heard the shot.

"Mike, look after Jenny and the boy!"

He raced off through the hangars, his battered ribs aching with the exertion, and when he reached the barracks saw Jacko on the ground and knelt beside him.

"Jacko!"

"'Ullo, Boss. Can you bloody believe it? Twenty years a soldier, never a scratch, now this," he said, wincing as the blood flowed through his fingers clutching his side.

"Is it bad?"

"It bloody 'urts! But I'm okay; don't think it 'it anythin' important. But I'll tell you what 'urts more."

"What's that?"

"I didn't bloody see 'im!"

A soldier's pride. Wilcox understood.

"You be all right here by yourself?" he asked.

Jacko nodded. "Give 'im one for me."

"Count on it."

"You'd better 'ave this," the Cockney said, handing Wilcox his automatic. "Couldn't stop a sparrer with that Colt."

The sound of running feet behind them. Wilcox vanished down the path between the second and third buildings. Behind him lay a frightened wife and child and the man who had saved his life in Ulster and before him was the bastard who would pay for it all with a life that would be ruthlessly taken from him.

At last he had reached the open ground. Reilly checked behind him and, seeing no sign of pursuit, began the painful lurching journey to the trees. His breath came laboured, each step he took made him shiver with agony. His gait was clumsy. He could hardly see, his vision impaired by the racking pain of the wound in the left side of his face.

Forty yards ... Thirty ... Twenty-five ...

Something behind him and he turned to see Peter Wilcox gaining on him. He fired, missed and fired again; then he was running once more. The blood pounded in his ears and his lungs felt like they would burst. Ten yards ... Five ... Then he had reached the woodland, was clawing at the fence.

A shot. The force of the bullet spun him round to face his pursuer. Fresh pain lanced through his body, through his left shoulder, he could barely lift his arm, the only arm he had left to defend himself with. He screamed with the pain. Screamed like an animal. Then he tried to raise his pistol and another bullet tore through his chest. He coughed. Vomited blood. Began to choke and collapsed on to his side, his right leg bent beneath him.

And then he heard a voice.

"Just so you know, I never did know who Perseus was. So you see, you died for nothing you son of a bitch."

The men from Special Branch heard the final shot and ran from the barracks to find Peter Wilcox walking towards them. They took his weapon and, two detectives continuing their run towards the dead Tim Reilly, escorted him to the area before the control tower where he joined Jenny and David and the others who were under supervision.

Jamie Daniels wandered over the killing ground. Stopping by Kelly, he looked at the dead man, at the horrible wound, then turned away before he vomited. His quiet office-life with MI5 had never prepared him for anything like this and he was suddenly thankful Thomson had denied him permission to transfer to the department in Belfast where sights such as this were commonplace.

What Thomson would make of all this, God only knew! Although he hadn't had the time to marshall all the facts, Daniels had learned about Jenny and David's abduction and the rescue which had been effected by Wilcox and his men. Had there been no killing it could probably have been hushed up. But now ...? He shook his head. You couldn't keep a thing like this under wraps.

Two terrorists dead. Another on his way to hospital where he would undergo an immediate operation to see if his testicles could be saved. Jacko Tyler also on his way to hospital with a bullet lodged dangerously near his kidneys. He would survive; so would Seamie McGee. But the whole bloody lot of them would probably end up in prison.

It was odd, but he felt guilty, somehow responsible. If he hadn't suggested keeping Wilcox under protective surveillance they would all have walked away free.

And then a thought occurred to him. If the surveillance were forgotten it might be possible to write the whole thing off as just another unsolved incident. It was certainly worth suggesting. Of course, it would have been a whole lot cleaner if *all* the terrorists had died. With one surviving, any attempt at a cover-up could prove embarrassing; but there were ways to persuade a man into silence, either by using bribery, promising a reduction in sentence in return for silence, or by threatening him with an increased sentence to be served in a place where his safety would not be guaranteed.

For a moment he was shocked by his cynicism, by his natural ability to entertain a reasoning which involved the manipulation of people and events to achieve an expedient goal. But was it really natural, or had it been acquired? That was something he was going to have to think about; and turning, he walked back to the cars which were preparing to depart.

CHAPTER 26

JOE Daley's farmhouse was built of weathered stone and chipped grey slate. It was situated in a remote clearing in a pine forest half-a-mile from the Lough and could be reached from the main road by a winding track which culminated in a gravelled forecourt bordered by a low brick wall. It was a good place for a meeting. It was quiet and protected from casual observation by the surrounding woodland and, in the event that flight should prove necessary, there were two available escape routes. Both could be found at the rear of the house: the first, a long and narrow track which was wide enough to take a car; and the second, a descending pathway leading through the trees to a powered craft moored sixty yards from the pebbled shore of the Lough.

It was a rural area with very little contact. Five miles to the east was Mulligan's farm, a smallholding of twenty-five acres which had been divided into three fields: one for growing potatoes, another for hay, while the land bordering the main road had been given over to a few head of cattle. To the north beyond the approach road were a further fifteen acres of arable land and timber belonging to another farmer who lived beyond the rise.

The meeting was to take place in the sitting room. The G-plan furniture had been shifted to make space for the long wooden table from the kitchen. Twelve chairs had been placed around the table and six bottles of Irish whiskey stood on a tin tray in the centre.

Martin Kennedy was studying the room in silence when the first car arrived. The light from its headlamps washed over his face as it rolled to a halt before the entrance. A moment later, he heard the slamming of doors and feet crunching across the gravel to the porch. He drained his glass, then nodded to Donal Brady who walked out into the hallway to answer the door.

Wheelan had been first through the vehicle checkpoint. There were five soldiers: the one who had waved them down; two lying prone in the bushes; one crouching ten yards away beside a low bridge spanning the river, holding one end of a long spiked chain designed to destroy the tyres of any vehicle attempting to drive through without stopping; and one seated in the cab of a jeep containing the radio.

"Is this your vehicle, sir?" the soldier asked. The driver nodded. "Then you won't mind showing me your documents, will you?"

As the driver reached across to the glove-box, the soldier flashed his torch across the faces of the two men seated in the back.

"Good evening, gentlemen," he said. "May I see some identification?"

Wheelan and the other man handed him their papers and, when the driver had supplied his licence and vehicle documentation, the soldier crossed to the trucks where he processed the information by radio. A few minutes later, he returned.

"Anything naughty in the boot?"

"Take a look," the driver replied.

The soldier nodded to one of his companions lying at the side of the road who checked and shook his head.

"Right, gentlemen," the soldier said, returning their papers and stepping aside. "Have a pleasant evening."

He waved to the soldier with the chain who dragged it off the road and the car drove away across the bridge.

Captain Daniel West and Trooper Shaw, 22 SAS, had watched the car arrive. They were lying concealed in the undergrowth in the woodland above the track and had been there for twenty-one hours. Sergeant Lofthouse and three others were in position at the rear of the farmhouse near the pathway to the Lough. They were the vanguard of Operation Trawler, a two-hundred-and-twenty man tactical force whose mission was to rescue Perseus and capture the Provo hierarchy; and it was their job to neutralize hostility in the Sterile Zone.

West spoke into his radio. "Lofty?"

"Go ahead, Boss."

"Guests arriving."

"Roger. Out."

Through his night-sight, West saw Wheelan enter the farmhouse and the driver crawl beneath the car where he removed two Armalite rifles. He watched him pass one to his companion; then they separated, moving out of sight as they took up their positions.

Frank Davis was sitting in a landrover parked beside the Temporary Operations Base concealed in the woodland three miles away. He had only arrived an hour ago, but already he was bored with waiting for the action to start. Colonel Harris of G1 Intelligence, a tall thin man with a wispy brown moustache, appeared and offered him a swig from his flask of brandy. Davis took it gratefully, wincing as the liquid burnt its way down to his ample belly, then returned it with a nod of thanks to the soldier who shoved it back inside his greatcoat pocket.

Reports came over the radio-net. One by one the cars arrived and, by eight o'clock, every member of PIRA's General Staff had entered the Sterile Zone. The order was given and, as troops began to close in from their positions in Mulligan's fields and the surrounding woodland, the RUC blocked both ends of the approach road.

It had started.

"One of us?" Wheelan asked incredulously. "Ye have t'be kiddin'!"

They were sitting round the long table, their tense faces lighted by the single shaded 60 watt bulb hanging above them. The room already smelled sour with the mixture of whiskey and sweat poorly masked by cheap deodorant, and a hovering wreath of cigarette smoke hung like a shroud on the charged air.

Kennedy was sitting in shadow at the head of the table.

"We're the only ones with access t'the kind o'detailed information the Brits've been actin' on," he said.

He studied the faces before him. Keegan, McCann, Gallagher the cripple, Wheelan and Donovan were on his left; and on his right were Brigade Commanders Gerry Kavanagh, Jim O'Hara, Danny Malahide, Rory Maguire and Paddy Lynch. Before him, at the bottom of the table, was Dermot O'Shea; while behind him, standing silent in the shadows with his arms folded, was Donal Brady.

"How can ye be sure we're not jumpin' through hoops?" Maguire asked. "Look at that business back in '79."

The Brits had skilfuly framed five middle-ranking members of the Movement and the Army Council of the day had ordered their executions. They had later been discovered in public thoroughfares with their knee-caps smashed and their tongues ripped out: a brutal warning to anyone else considering betrayal.

"T'hell with '79!" Kennedy snapped. "Look at the facts! Their clean-up rate proves conclusively that we've been compromised!"

"I still think ye're barkin' up the wrong tree," Keegan said hesitantly. "We're all too committed."

"Commitment can be bought or compromised," the Chief replied. "An' has been in the past."

"But not at our level," Wheelan said.

"Nine years is enough time t'climb the ladder."

Gallagher coughed and leaned forward in his wheelchair, his voice rasping like a blunt saw. "The Movement can't stand another witch hunt, Martin. We'd never recover."

"An' we're losin' our status as it is," Donovan said. "One wrong step an' we're finished."

"We're damn near finished anyway," Paddy Lynch snarled. "Our operations have practically been brought to a standstill an' we're losin' men in the field."

"S'right," said Kavanagh, "I've lost seven in the past six months."

"An' I've lost five," Malahide said. "Two dead, three doin' time in the Kesh."

"An' with all that ye still think we're as pure as Snow White's arse?" Kennedy asked. "No lads; someone in this room's a traitor. An' no one bloody leaves here till he's found ..."

Captain West was staring into his scope. There were sixteen armed guards prowling the grounds and the luminous dial of his wristwatch told him there were fifteen minutes to go before the order came through to move in.

He checked his automatic pistol, then his MP5. Despite the low temperature, his blackened face was beaded with sweat and for the thousandth time he ran over the order of assault. Two waves, front and rear, knock out the guards, enter and secure the farmhouse and call in the result. Should any escape, and it was likely some would, Operation Trawler would commence and they would net them. Sounded easy, but West was experienced enough to know how large the gulf was between a plan and its successful execution. They called the gulf The Buggeration Factor, for if one small thing had been overlooked – if one of the cogs refused to turn – the whole machine would grind to a halt and the resulting chaos could only be dangerous.

Back at the Temporary Operations Base, Frank Davis was visibly nervous. Even though he had no part to play in the assault he felt the tension of anticipation fused with the surrounding activity.

"Soon be over," Colonel Frost reassured him. "About bloody time we had a break like this. I'm sick to death of pissing about with my hands tied. If I had my way I'd just shoot the buggers."

"Isn't that just what you're intending to do?" Davis asked.

"Good Lord, no! We're the good guys!" He chuckled. "Mind you, those SAS boys walk a pretty thin line. They'll give the bleeding hearts a case to cry about. You know, State Terrorism, that kind of thing, but the majority'll lap it up."

Davis nodded. Ever since the rescue of the hostages in the Iranian embassy, the Special Air Service had personified pride to a nation which was tired of being sneered at. To many, they were a symbol of the qualities which had made Britain great and their ruthless professionalism was admired throughout the world.

Frost offered him his flask, but he declined. He wanted to stay clear, to take it all in. The soldier took a healthy swig, then clapped him on the back.

"Soon be over," he repeated. "And then it's back to the paperwork and bollocks."

"Every decision we reach is passed along the chain o'command," Maguire protested. "What makes ye so sure the leak isn't there?"

"For Christ's sake!" Kennedy barked. "If ye'd bloody well listened t'what I've been sayin', ye'd know why!"

Maguire paled beneath the Chief's withering glare and looked nervously round the table for support. There wasn't any.

"The ASU's are cellular. They don't know what the other Brigades are up to. Which leaves us. We're the ones who hold the strings. We make the decisions. Which means that one of us is the tout."

Every man felt the tension. Guarded looks were exchanged and eyes averted when the stares of suspicion became too intense.

"Okay," said O'Hara, "let's say ye're right. Let's say one of us has betrayed the Movement. Jus' how d'ye propose findin' out which one of us it is? I mean, it's a bit bloody unlikely he'll jus' throw up his hand an' admit it."

A murmer of assent and Kennedy slapped the table-top to quell it.

"Donal?"

Brady cleared his throat and paused before stepping from the shadows. He could barely control the terror he felt, the sickening fear which made him want to flee. But he knew he had to play the game to its end, that in a few minutes he would be safe, that he would soon be far away. Every man's eye was upon him and he found to his surprise that, when he spoke, his voice was steady.

"Every man here has secrets," he said. "Classic material for a hostile approach." He looked at Donovan. "Proddie mistresses." Then at Wheelan. "Other men's wives. Leverage which could be used by the Brits t'get information."

"Jesus!" cried Donovan. "Ye've been havin' us watched!"

The room resounded in angry protest. Each man voiced his indignation and the tension soon gave way to bitter quarrelling. Donovan turned to O'Shea releasing all his bilious hatred, accusing the Provo Finance Officer of selling-out to the Brits for money and the smaller man leapt to his feet.

"I've taken enough o'your bullshit!" he cried.

"Will ye be wantin' t'settle this now?" the big man asked, his heavy face quivering with ugly anticipation. "Or maybe wait till later when the boys aren't here t'see ye flattened?"

"Well, it's not bloody me!" Wheelan shouted defensively to no one in particular.

Keegan seemed to be having trouble focussing and he tore the pebble glasses from his nose and wiped them clean on his tie.

Gerry Kavanagh's freckled hands slammed down on the table punctuating his denial, and Gallagher the cripple vigorously rubbed the stubs which had once been his legs as he smashed them into the table in his effort to wheel himself nearer.

"I lost me fuckin' legs fightin' for the Cause!" he cried. "Some fuckin' tout with no fuckin' legs!"

"Ye've still got a mouth!" Lynch replied nastily and set his teeth against the heated response.

"An' ye're only half-Irish, anyway," Donovan was goading and O'Shea lost his customary cool.

"That's it! That's bloody well it!"

He leapt across the table, his hands reaching out to the big man's throat and, as they grappled, the whiskey bottles smashed to the floor. The Chief's face was suddenly suffused with rage and he jumped to his feet.

"Donovan!"

As if by magic the room fell silent.

"Are you the tout, Michael Donovan?"

"Me? No! Christ, Martin, ye know me – ye've known me for years! I'm ..."

"That Proddy whore o'yours was married to a Branch man!"

Donovan had known that; it had been part of the buzz.

Every eye was upon him, some curious, others hostile, and he tore his collar open, the button flying off onto the table where he looked at it stupidly. Kennedy was playing a long shot, with no proof that Donovan was the informer; but the pieces were there – the material for compromise was there – and he had been privy to every single soured operation.

The silence coiled around the big man like a serpant, choking off the air, making it hard for him to breathe, making him sweat. He saw the hatred in his compatriots' eyes, felt the terror rise and then came the anger, deep, burning, resentful of being unjustly accused, of being suspected.

He roared.

"Look out!" Wheelan cried; and O'Hara, who could match him in size, leapt up and took hold of him. Others joined in and, in the struggle, Donovan was viciously clubbed to the floor and battered senseless.

"Get him to his chair!" Kennedy ordered.

"What'll we do with him?" asked Keegan.

"I say we nut the bastard!" Gallagher snarled.

General agreement, although there were some who thought a bullet too quick for the sodding tout.

"I've a drill in the car," Lynch offered.

All eyes turned to Kennedy, looking for a sign, an order. When it came, it was little more than a tired whisper.

"Take him out t'the barn," he said; and as O'Hara and Wheelan stooped to pick Donovan up, the door swung open and Sean O'Malley walked in.

CHAPTER 27

THE signal was given, a single word of command which crackled over the radio. West jumped to his feet, moved fast through the foliage towards the forecourt, Trooper Shaw and another two soldiers fanning out behind him in a line. At the rear of the farmhouse, Sergeant Lofthouse and his team simultaneously broke cover. There were five armed guards who didn't even have time to turn around. They were taken out with precision and speed; a sharp blow to the back of the head with a gun butt and plastic handcuffs to secure them for the back-up.

"What the hell's goin' on?" Kennedy demanded.

O'Malley ignored him. "Surprised t'see me, Donal?"

Brady didn't reply; no one moved, all staring uncomprehendingly at the strange scene unfolding before them.

O'Malley moved to the table and poured himself a whiskey, grimacing as the amber liquid bit.

"What's your business here, Sean?" Kennedy asked.

"My business?" He put his glass down on the table and gazed at Donovan slumped unconscious in his chair. "What's up with him?"

"He's a bastard tout," O'Hara said. "We're fixin' t'give him a send-off."

"That a fact?"

"Been squealin' t'the Brits for years, so he has. Even gave him a code-name."

"Perseus?"

"How the hell did ye know that?" Kennedy asked.

"Why don't ye ask Donal?"

Suddenly, everything was falling to pieces. Brady felt his bowels churn, felt a cold sweat prick his flesh and raised a trembling hand to wipe his face.

Silence. Every eye was upon him. O'Malley poured himself another drink and watched him expressionlessly over the rim of the tumbler.

Frank Davis banged his head on the roof of the landrover as it sped along the brake.

"Sorry about that, sir," said the Intelligence corporal at the wheel.

"Never mind bloody grinning," Davis snapped, "just watch where you're going!"

Another pothole; they landed with a crash and a skid, and the MI5 man, holding tight to the edge of his seat, prayed it would soon be over.

"Is this true?" Kennedy asked.

O'Malley had explained how Brady had sent him to the mainland to kill Peter Wilcox; and Donal, almost rooted with fear, violently shook his head.

"No!"

"Sean?" the Chief said.

O'Malley didn't reply. Beside him, Donovan stirred, his bloodied face wincing as returning consciousness brought back the pain. Kennedy looked back at Donal Brady, uncertainty lining his face.

"Are you the tout?" he asked, not wanting to believe it. But before he could get a response the door crashed open and one of the guards lurched in, blood dripping from a nasty gash in the side of his head and his rifle held out for balance.

"Fuckin' place is surrounded!" he cried, his voice underlined by the sudden eruption of gunfire; and Donal, taking quick advantage of the distraction, slipped out through the door and away through the gathering darkness.

West's team engaged the guards in the forecourt, rolling like acrobats and using the parked cars for cover. Trooper Shaw was moving across the yard when a figure raced out of the farmhouse and across to the perimeter wall.

"Stop!" he commanded.

Donal, who had drawn his pistol, loosed off a flurry of wild shots, one of which thumped into the soldier's chest spinning him round and knocking him to the ground, then leapt over the low wall and vanished into the trees.

Lofthouse, meanwhile, had led his team in through the back, kicking the door open and surprising a lone guard who didn't even have time to raise his weapon. Lofthouse's burst punched through him and lifted him into the wall. He was dead before he hit the ground.

They kept on moving, splitting into pairs and kicking doors open as they went. The sounds of gunfire and percussion grenades rent the air as they took out all signs of opposition. Finally, they reached the front room. Lofthouse put his shoulder to the door and immediately dropped flat when he saw Paddy Lynch, arms extended, aiming a handgun. The bullet thwacked into the wall above him and, before the skinny Brigade

Commander could squeeze off another round, Trooper Grundy dived in through the doorway and riddled him with his MP5.

"All of you, face down on the floor! Move!"

The Provo General Staff obeyed with alacrity. Lofthouse jumped to his feet and covered them while his team secured them with plastic tape.

The building was secured.

Out in the forecourt, West put his head out of cover and was met by a furious burst of automatic fire. The bodywork of the car bucked as the bullets ripped into it with a metallic ping and a tyre burst with a loud hiss. He ducked back and found a frightened guard had materialized beside him, trembling weapon levelled at his head. Working by instinct, West spun aside and, just as the youth's finger tightened on the trigger, put a quarter-clip into his torso and the terrorist dropped at his feet.

One of the cars revved into life, headlamps lighting the killing ground. The IRA man threw it into gear and stamped on the accelerator, exhaust fumes fouling the chill night air, and, as the car shot forward, a trooper broke cover and loosed off a full clip which shattered the windscreen. The car slewed and the soldier dived to one side. Out of control, it slammed into the low perimeter wall, almost overturning as it pivoted on the displaced brickwork, its horn blaring harshly in the night.

And then, as suddenly as it had begun, it ended. Sergeant Lofthouse strode out of the building and found West standing grimly over the body of Trooper Shaw. The boy had only been with the Regiment for three months, had been a popular addition to the Squadron; and Lofthouse could see the officer was holding back, trying to stay in control of his emotions.

"Lofty?"

"Boss?"

"All secured?"

"Tight as a drum."

"Call it in, then come back and deal with this lot," West said, nodding to the knot of surrendered gunmen sitting on the gravel.

As Lofthouse went to radio the TOB, Trooper Grundy walked to the car and, yanking open the door, reached under the driving wheel and ripped out a bunch of wires to disconnect the horn. It took a moment for the silence to register; a harsh, vibrant emptiness filling the void created by the cessation of action.

"Schooner, this is Marlin One. Please respond. Over."

The Signals private leaned out through the back of the radio truck and called Colonel Boyd, the Ops Commander, who was chatting with Colonel Harris.

"Contact, sir."

Boyd jumped inside and took the microphone. "Marlin One, this is Schooner. What is your situation? Over."

"Sterile Zone secured. Send QRF and medical assistance."

Boyd turned and waved to the Field Support Team who set off down the track at speed.

"On their way, Marlin One. Have you Perseus?"

"Negative Schooner. Perseus made off when the action started. Am informed their Player in hostile pursuit. Suggest you activate net. Out."

The Ops Commander returned the microphone to the private.

"Contact Fleet. Tell them to proceed with the trawl."

As he returned to Harris, the soldier intoned: "Schooner to Fleet. Commence trawl. Repeat. Commence trawl."

A line of soldiers crouching in the bushes marking the boundary of Mulligan's farm stood up and made their way into the woodland. When they reached the trees, they fanned out and were quickly swallowed up by the darkness.

The first thing Donal had done when he ran into cover was to catch his breath. He hadn't meant to shoot that soldier. It had been an instinctive thing. When a few seconds had passed and he had drawn breath he had pushed off through the pinewood. He could have stayed and given himself up to the people who had been sent in to find him, but his adrenalin had been pumping and the urge to run was so intense that he had only wanted to get as far away from the farmhouse as possible.

Sean O'Malley had also managed to get away. When the shooting had started, he had made his way to an upstairs bedroom and had let himself out through the window. He had seen Donal disappearing into the woodland and had waited for the action to move to another part of the yard before taking off in pursuit.

Released by the arrival of the Quick Reaction Force, West collected his men and they melted into the pinewood. Although the net had been activated, there was no guarantee it would succeed in reaching Perseus before the Player who pursued him. Sergeant Lofthouse had persuaded one of the Provos to tell them where the escape routes lay and, since the track running across country fell within the immediate area of the trawl, West had decided to lead his men to the Lough.

It had started to rain. Donal clawed his way up a steep slope and, reaching the top, paused to get his bearings. Seventy yards away to the east, a soldier saw him framed in the moonlight and ordered him to stand fast. He swung round in surprise and, as he started to bolt, a shot rang out, the bullet tearing through his arm and the impact hurled him down the other side of the slope where he fetched up with a loud grunt against the rough bark of a pine tree.

O'Malley heard the shot and stopped. It had come from his right and, quickly changing direction, he ploughed off through the undergrowth in pursuit. The rough brush snagged at the cuffs of his trousers, the path was slippery in the rain, and he cursed as once, twice, he lost his purchase, cutting his hand as he reached out to steady himself.

In a way it seemed unreal tracking a man he had known so well for the purpose of killing him. O'Malley had always been too much of a loner to make easy friendships; but when Donal had protected his brother from the vengeance of those he had betrayed, he had felt the burden of gratitude and a liking for the man. But when Brady had blackmailed him into going across the water by threatening exposure of his brother's betrayal, his emotive response had been blocked by the necessity of removing the threat and now, released from his sense of obligation, there was only the prey and the inevitability of extinction.

Frank Davis also followed the sound of the shot. Out of condition, he laboured through the pinewood. Shouts. Another shot. God, would it never end? Cursing, he groped his way up the slope taking hold of the trees; and then, with a cry, he tripped and fell headlong into the dip.

Donal could feel the warm blood pulsing through his cotton sleeve and down to his hand. His breathing came in racking gasps and he sobbed with pain as he stumbled down the path to the shoreline.

The water shimmered like black glass and the chill breeze swept the driving rain into his face. He could see the ketch bobbing rhythmically on the windswept surface, could see the slim mast rising from the body of the boat like a beckoning finger. Wiping a rat-tail of hair from his eye, he urged himself on towards the row boat beached ten feet from the water's edge and collapsed with exhaustion when he reached it.

The bullet had just missed O'Malley as he gathered his footing on the rise. Ducking instinctively, he had tumbled down the grassy bank to the track his quarry had taken to the Lough. His breathing frosted in the moonlight and he spat away the phlegm which came from smoking too many cigarettes. Then, thirty yards away he saw Donal Brady reach and fall beside the row boat; and, drawing breath and the Walther pistol from his pocket, lumbered over the shale towards him.

Close behind him Captain West and his troopers appeared silhouetted on the skyline. Scanning the shore, West's arm shot out.

"Over there!" he cried.

Frank Davis, soaked to the skin and muddied from his fall, heard the shout and veered towards it. His breath rasped and his flabby muscles ached with the effort of unfamiliar exercise. Christ, he was tired, wanted to stop; but he didn't; kept on moving, tired legs leaden as he ran through the pain.

With a final desperate effort Donal began to haul the small craft over the rainwashed pebbles towards the lapping water. The pain coursed through his wounded arm as the numbness of shock began wearing off and he fought the nausea which threatened to overwhelm him with every movement, every step he took. Then the water was tugging at his ankles. A few more feet and he would feel the boat being lifted from the bed.

"Donal!"

He swung round in surprise, losing his balance and splashing clumsily backwards into the water. He hadn't heard O'Malley approach and struggled to maintain his hold on the boat. Behind O'Malley he could see a group of soldiers sliding down the rise towards them. If he could only keep him talking till they arrived he might be in with a chance.

"Jesus, Sean, can ye not see it's over? Drop your gun or the bloody soldiers'll kill ye."

"Why'd ye do it, Donal" Why'd ye turn tout?"

"They had me by the balls. I'd no choice. Jus' like your brother, Danny." He coughed, turned away, his finger curling round the grip of his pistol. "Ye owe me, Sean. For Danny. Ye owe me his life. Ye know what would've happened if Kennedy had got hold o'him. I'm askin' ye, Sean, t'let it go. Jus' turn away. There's been enough killin'. Don't push it any more."

O'Malley shook his head. "It's too late, Donal. Ye called the tune, now it's time t'pay the piper."

He raised his pistol. Donal drew his. O'Malley started to move, to dive away, but he was too late, Brady's bullet catching him high up in the chest. As he fell, he fired and the shot smashed into Donal's head. The impact knocked him back against the boat, rocking it off the bottom of the Lough and out into the rippling water.

The SAS men finally reached them. Sergeant Lofthouse knelt beside O'Malley. He was barely breathing and a thin line of blood ran from his mouth where it glistened on the shale. West and Grundy waded into the water and pulled Donal Brady to the shore and, as they laid him down, Frank Davis arrived and fell to his knees beside him.

For nearly a decade Brady had supplied the security forces with information. Caught, turned, forced into betraying his people, his friends, his beliefs, he had been left out in the cold, abandoned because of the vanity of one man who had died without arranging his deliverance.

To have come this far, thought Davis, and to die on the cusp of his rescue. Christ, it was a joke, a cruel and bloody sick joke.

He turned and was violently sick. One of the troopers helped him to his feet and he stared down at the corpse, no longer conscious of the rain which lashed his face.

All he knew was that the man codenamed Perseus was dead, that they had failed in their promise to look after him.

EPILOGUE

HARRY Thomson looked down through his shatterproof office window on to Curzon Street. A line of motorcycles was parked before the jutting concrete parapet designed to ward off an explosion and, apart from a few pedestrians hurrying past in the rain, the street was deserted.

Five days had passed since Operation Trawler had failed in its objective to rescue the compromised informer. Had they succeeded in pulling Brady out alive, his knowledge regarding the murderous activities of PIRA's General Staff would, if he had agreed to testify, have justified the enormous expense of sending a 220- strong attack force into the field. But since he had been killed and the authorities did not have enough evidence to convict them, they had been released for the law was such that they could not be charged with terrorist offences without proof. It was the system. But something good had come of it. Sources in Ulster had reported that the Movement was in turmoil, that the Hard Men had been discredited. Things would quieten down for a short time, but Thomson knew they would only be replaced and that the violence would continue as before, would probably escalate as the Organization strove to regain its credibility.

Releasing the slat in the blind he returned to his desk and scanned the updated Gorgon file. It was hard to believe that a mere three weeks had passed since Perseus had first come to his attention. All the pieces were now in place, the jigsaw was completed; he had even received a fax from Colonel Harris which tied an Intelligence corporal into place as the source of the Perseus leak. Apparently Christy Keegan, the Sinn Fein councillor, had informed on him and now the soldier was safely under arrest.

Tall oaks from little acorns grow. And spread, he thought, remembering how the men involved in the conception of Operation Gorgon had been hunted down, a hunt which had ended bloodily at the airfield in Apstead.

After consultation, it had been decided at the highest level to take no action against Peter Wilcox and his team. The police had issued a statement accepting full responsibility for the action and, if the terrorist McGee attempted to set the record straight by getting word to the Press about what had really happened, he would find himself being transferred to a prison where his safety would most certainly be overlooked and a 'D' notice would be issued preventing disclosure.

Jacko Tyler, the man who had saved Peter Wilcox's life in South Armagh, had undergone immediate surgery to remove the bullet which had lodged near his kidneys. The operation had taken three-and-a-quarter hours and he was now recuperating in a private hospital in Berkshire, his condition described as comfortable.

After their ordeal, the Wilcox family had gone to Wales. Jamie Daniels had been to visit them in Lindfield with the news that the authorities were not going to press any charges. Naturally, the ordeal they had been through had affected Jenny and their son; but there had been talk of a reconciliation and the break was part of the process.

It was amazing how the act of betrayal had affected so many lives.

Moira Brady had not only lost her husband, but had also been driven from her house by vengeful neighbours. The security forces had arrived at the scene to find her watching helplessly as fire destroyed their lives and their possessions. The fire brigade had been stung by missiles and abuse and the situation had necessitated reinforcing the soldiery as they tried to control the mob. Very little was rescued from the blaze and Moira and the kids had been taken into protective custody while arrangements were being made to resettle them.

Frank Davis, who had been William Tyndall's link with Donal Brady, had resigned from the Service having given his report of Operation Trawler to the DG. He had been sickened by the whole affair and planned to buy a farm in Bedfordshire where he had been raised. Anyone less suited to farmwork than Davis, Thomson could not imagine; but he understood his need to break away.

Though Davis would have denied it, Trawler was merely the culmination of a disgust which had been building for some time. Officers new to MI5 saw nothing but the glamour of being 'in the know'; but when the glaze wore off and they saw the imperfections, the seamy side of the work, many became disenchanted, questioning the morality of what they did, and walked away before the damage was so great that every last shred of humanity had been stripped from them. The Northern Ireland experience accelerated the process, and Davis, who had served there longer than most, was just another casualty in a soul- destroying war of attrition.

There was a knock on the door and Jamie Daniels entered with a batch of files which he dropped on the desk. Even he had been affected by the events of the last three weeks, losing his exuberance, and his ready smile was strained and unconvincing.

'I'll see you on Monday, sir."

"All right, Jamie. Goodnight."

The door closed and Thomson, shaking his head, hoped the damage had not gone too deep.

The weekend.

Closing the Gorgon file and slipping it into the out-tray, he took a look at the top file on the ones Daniels had delivered. The randy Cabinet Minister, the Press had found proof regarding his sexual indiscretions, the PM had been livid, the minister resigned and, three days later the whole affair was still front page material.

Thomson knocked the dottle from his pipe, pocketed it, then rose and collected his raincoat. Monica Tyndall had invited him to spend the weekend at Chardonay and, turning out the light, he left his office and wandered slowly down the corridor to the lift and thought no more of Operation Gorgon and the man his predecessor codenamed Perseus.